HITMAN WEDDING

EVE LANGLAIS

CHAPTER ONE

SOMEONE HAD KILLED STEFANOV. WHILE NOT A NICE man, or a close friend, her temporary partner didn't deserve to lie in a pool of cooling blood. More disturbing, Francesca would likely be killed next, unless she escaped. Options for said escape, however, were quite limited.

The room she found herself in didn't have many egresses. The patio doors led to a balcony overhanging a seaside cliff, currently whipped by a tropical storm. While agile and fit, she wasn't about to climb the slick, rocky face. A locked door leading out to the main area of the house taunted, but she didn't take the bait. It wasn't any safer out there.

There's a killer on the island. Someone with an unknown agenda.

With her two main exits crossed out, it left only one option, a poor one at that. She took the spiral stairs in the far corner of the room. They coiled upwards to a rooftop deck where safety was but an illusion as the storm buffeted the island situated off the Florida Keys. Wind whipped her skin and pelted her with raindrops. It soaked and chilled to the bone, but she didn't let the poor conditions distract her. When the woman chasing her emerged from below, she was ready.

"Keep away." Francesca snarled the warning, her gun aimed at Kacy's face.

The petite Latina with a cool composure probably inherited from a cat, didn't look daunted at all to be facing down the barrel of a gun. "I'm not here to kill you. Just making sure you aren't planning to shoot Darren." Darren being Kacy's boss. And Francesca's ex-lover.

"I should. It would make things easier." So much so if all Francesca needed was to shoot him. "He wasn't supposed to be here. He ruined everything." Ruined it with his angry glares—and reminders of a time when those lips used to purse in pleasure, not disdain.

"What's wrong? Did your new boyfriend not like the one you dumped showing up?" The wind snatched the words from Kacy's mouth, but the woman stood close enough for Francesca to hear them.

"You don't understand. No one does. There's more at stake than you know."

"Then perhaps you should explain."

How to make clear that she had no choice? "I was trying, but then Stefanov arrived. He didn't take kindly to Darren's treatment of me." A well-deserved harangue, given what she'd done to him. Some men had a hard time letting go.

"Was that the plan all along? To have Stefanov lure Darren to this island so he could kill him?"

"What? Of course not." If Francesca wanted Darren dead, she'd do it herself. "You shouldn't speculate on things you know nothing about."

"I know that someone is trying to kill Darren, and right about now, you and Stefanov seem like the most likely suspects."

Stefanov might have had his own agenda, but her? "I'm not trying to kill him." She might be the only one other than Kacy who wasn't.

"Weren't you the one claiming the killer was on this island? How else would you know unless it's you or your new boyfriend?"

The conversation was going nowhere, and Francesca recognized it for what it was. A stalling tactic. She kept her gun steady even when startled by the arrival of a new player.

"Francesca isn't the one behind the murder attempts." Darren's voice cut through the storm —cold, angry.

She didn't even think about it, simply angled the gun away from Kacy and pointed it at Darren.

Not one of her brightest moves.

The petite Kacy wasn't one to waste an opportunity. She lunged forward, thrusting out and punching Francesca in the tit. It shocked more than it hurt and drew a gasp from Francesca. Her fingers loosened enough that Kacy knocked the gun from her hand.

But Francesca didn't retaliate. Didn't wipe the smug

smirk off Kacy's face, mostly because she knew that fighting wouldn't win her this battle.

His face a stony mask, Darren moved until he stood between them. "I'll take over from here."

"Go ahead. Toss her over the side." Kacy waited for Darren to act, and Francesca wondered if his anger was great enough to do it. To actually murder her in cold blood.

I don't think he will. Not the Darren she knew. That man was a lover, not a killer.

Darren shook his head. "I'm not killing her yet. I need to speak with Fran. Alone, please."

Kacy sputtered. "The girl just had a gun pointed at you. You can't seriously expect me to go."

"I do."

"What about her boyfriend?"

Stefanov wouldn't be coming to her aid. Darren already knew that.

"Marcus took care of him. So you can leave us alone. I assure you, I can handle Fran by myself."

Yes, he certainly could. He had a knack for making her melt and do whatever he wanted—in the bedroom. But she doubted he was here to seduce her into giving him a second chance.

When Darren and Kacy turned to look at her, she made sure to look weak. Shaking in the pouring rain, hunched in on herself. She even managed to bat her damp lashes and let her lower lip tremble.

The fine act didn't fool Kacy for a second. "She's fucking with you."

Smart girl.

Darren didn't budge. "Leave, Kacy. That's an order."

The urge to stick out her tongue was strong, but Francesca kept her lips clamped as Kacy walked away muttering, "If she kills you, expect me to say I told you so."

Except Francesca wasn't planning to kill Darren, no matter what outside forces wanted. The bigger question was, what would Darren do with her?

"I'm scared," she stated, trying to be the person he expected. Weak and afraid, a woman who needed a man to take care of her.

For a moment, his expression softened, just a flicker before he shuttered it. "Bullshit. I don't think you're scared at all."

"Stefanov is dead. Murdered."

"Did you do it?"

The very question had her mouth rounding and an indignant "No!" spitting from her lips. "You said your man did it. Killed him in cold blood."

"Actually, I don't know who killed your *boyfriend*." Said with a sneer.

"He's not my boyfriend." For some reason, it seemed important to clarify that.

"I really don't fucking care."

Words that shouldn't have hurt. "What do you want with me?"

"What do you think I want, Fran?"

For a moment, he let the anger shine through, so much resentment, and well deserved, too.

As Francesca stood on the rooftop, storm wind whipping at her hair, face-to-face with the man she used to sleep with, a guy she'd coldly rejected, her gun lying uselessly on the ground, she had to wonder how she'd gotten here.

Her boss, Sergei, being a bit of a smartass, would say, "*You took the stairs.*" The truth, however, was much more complicated.

The reason Francesca was here had to do with a mysterious invitation. Normal people didn't turn down a chance at a tropical vacation. Even deadly ones.

Since they were alone, she could at least speak freely. "You need to leave the island," she declared. "It's not safe."

He lifted his face to the sky overhead. "It's just a little tropical storm." Fat, wet drops soaked them while lightning lit up the sky.

"I'm not talking about the storm. I'm talking about the fact that this island is a trap."

"You don't say," Darren said flatly, his granite-like countenance rigid.

He was angry. Rightly so. She'd done something pretty cruel to him. Low even for her.

I made him love me. Then she'd left him.

"No matter your feelings for me, you have to listen."

"Why would I listen to you? You are obviously not who you said you were."

"I don't know what you mean."

"I mean that you're not a real model. Whom do you work for?"

She tried her best to appear innocent. "I don't know what you're implying."

"Yeah, you fucking do. Who the fuck are you? Other

than a lying cunt." He cursed at her, and she flinched from the harsh words then jumped again as lightning sizzled, followed by an immediate crack of thunder.

"I don't have to listen to this." When she moved, he grabbed her arm, painfully tight.

"Yeah, you do. Because I think you're involved with whatever is happening here. Did you kill Stefanov and the others?" By others, he meant the other guests on the luxury island.

"I've killed no one." Not today at least, and not since her arrival. But the day wasn't over yet.

"I don't believe you."

With good reason. "That is your choice. Don't say I didn't warn you that the island is a trap. I'm leaving." Before something regrettable happened. She yanked free and didn't look at her gun lying on the deck as she whirled, but she knew where it was as she started for the stairs.

"I can't let you leave, Fran."

"Then you'll have to stop me." She expected him to act. To attack her. What she'd not braced herself for was the soft query.

"Why, Fran? Why'd you do it? I thought we had something special."

They did, but falling for Darren hadn't been part of the plan. "Work called."

"And you couldn't stick around to explain or say goodbye?"

A glance over her shoulder showed him walking slowly toward her, the look on his face vulnerable. Soft. She turned away, unable to face him as she lied. "I didn't want to deal with the whining." A callous slap of words.

He sucked in a breath. "Nice to see what you really think of me."

Why did he sound so close?

She opened her eyes to see him right in front of her. She only had a second to register it before the needle entered her arm.

"What are you doing?"

"I told you, I want answers."

"You can't do this. I'm not here for you."

"Why *are* you here? Who sent you?"

Even if she wanted to, she couldn't reply. The world in front of her got blurry, her tongue thick as the lethargy took hold almost instantly. Her knees buckled. She slumped to the ground, yet didn't smash her face on it. She could have sworn arms cradled her, familiar and warm.

She turned into that heat and mumbled, "I've missed you."

To which he replied, "Liar."

CHAPTER TWO

LIAR, LIAR, PANTS ON FIRE. FOR SOME REASON, THAT song kept playing over and over in Darren's head. Ever since he'd captured Francesca.

More like kidnapped. This time, she wasn't running away.

You're not going anywhere until I get some answers.

Darren took his time tying Francesca to the chair. He wanted this moment to be just right. After all, he'd waited months for a chance to get his revenge. No point in rushing something that should be savored.

Fuck what anyone says. It does taste sweet.

As luck would have it, the yacht carried just the right tools. The wooden chair made for sunning on the deck that he'd pulled from a storage locker was a special surprise. Lots to admire in its sturdy teak construction, wide frame, and—best of all—perfectly placed slats. Plenty of places to loop rope to keep someone from moving.

I wouldn't want her to escape. We have so much to discuss.

Such as why she'd lied all those months ago.

The anger still burned hotly, as did the hotter shame that he hadn't caught on. Never realized as he sank into her willing flesh, her nails raking down his back, that she was planning to play him for a fool.

Now, who's the fool? He'd found her again, and she would answer for her actions.

In repose, her head leaned forward, her eyes still shut and her breathing even. The sedative he'd administered kept her asleep, stopped her from impeding his progress as he took her from the mansion—and in the nick of time before it exploded. When a home relied on propane for much of its utilities, it was easier than expected to blow it up.

Francesca slept through it. The sedation kept her from asking questions as he navigated the dark trails on the island, ignoring the sound of gunshots occasionally cracking behind them.

The quiet respite wouldn't last much longer, though. Darren pushed silken, damp, chestnut strands from her face, layering them over her shoulder so he could wrap the rope firmly around her upper body. Her clothes still bore the dampness of the storm they'd fled. The tempest that still raged outside—and within.

What a wet and wild run his escape to the yacht had proven to be. A few times, he'd questioned his sanity—especially as the lightning crashed, illuminating the darkness and giving it a nightmarish feel—but vengeance kept him going. The hot burn of his anger gave him strength to carry Fran, to cast off, and set them rocking in turbulent seas.

She slept the entire time, but she'd wake soon. He had to be ready.

He wound more rope around her upper body. The slide and tug of the nylon over her blouse brought a frisson to her skin. It affected him, as well.

Revenge could be so exciting. Almost sexual. Not that he would ever touch her in that way again—even if he still remembered the sweetness of her mouth.

Her lying lips.

She'd pay for what she did.

Pay for making a fool out of me.

It seemed as if Darren had waited forever for this chance. An eternity to discover what went wrong. Why did she do it? How could she drop him so callously? Not that he cared. Not anymore.

Now, he had another reason to hate—yet he still found himself stirred by the sweet curve of her cheek. Another reason, other than revenge, to question her.

She stirred, her long lashes fluttering against her pale skin, her body undulating as she tried to stretch her limbs and found them caught.

It brought to mind another time, another place. Her body, clad in only the thinnest of lingerie, spread and bound to four posts with silken scarves. Undulating with pleasure. Lips parted on the most musical of moans.

Now, those same lips pulled tautly in displeasure as Francesca realized she was a prisoner. Things changed since those naked days in France. For one,

Darren hated her. She was now but a tool in an ongoing mission. If only his body would listen. But no, he couldn't stem his arousal as he remembered how it felt to sink balls-deep into her.

Her brilliant blue eyes opened wide in shock. "Darren. What's happening?"

"Hello, Fran. Have a nice nap?"

She pulled, and her gaze narrowed. "Untie me at once."

He would.

Eventually.

But first, he held up a knife. "We need to talk."

"Are you seriously threatening me?"

He arched a brow. "Who's threatening? I haven't said a thing. I just want to chat. We've spent a few days on the island now"—an island he'd been brought to by devious means—"more or less avoiding each other." When she saw him coming, she turned the other way. "I thought...you know what, this is silly. Surely, as reasonable adults, we can discuss what happened."

"Reasonable?" She gave an intentional tug at her tethers as she glared. "Untie me."

"That's not what you said the last time." The last time he'd bound her, spread eagle on a bed, she'd moaned and screamed as he pleasured every inch of her body. That was months ago now. A mere blip in his past. He'd spent days on the island wondering if she now played the wanton prisoner for Stefanov.

Did she scream for him like she screamed for me?

"You have no idea what you're doing."

"Don't I?" He arched a brow. "I took hog tying as one of my electives."

Part of her control slipped, and she yelled. Eyes flashed. She snarled. "Release me at once."

She'd never looked sexier or angrier. Fascinating, because during their short time together, not once had he seen her lose her temper. She always had a ready smile or a boisterous laugh.

She wasn't laughing now. He'd finally given her a reason to be miffed. He had the upper hand. She was under his control. "I'm not letting you go." A lie. He would. Eventually. For now, she stayed because Darren needed answers, starting with a basic one. "What's your real name?" he asked, taking a spot across from her on the edge of the bed.

We rarely made it to a bed. The counter, floor, wall, couch, even in the backseat of a cab. The insane fever he used to have for her overcame any common sense.

"You know my name." She pulled at the rope, hands twisting, testing his knot. "What kind of sick game are you playing? Is this because you're still mad I left?"

She had disappeared. Without warning. Not one fucking word of goodbye.

"What makes you think I'm angry? You did me a favor. You proved what Marcus was saying all along. You played me." Made him look like a fool.

"How? I was interested. We dated. We fucked. I got bored. I left."

The words were thrown with nonchalance. If Darren didn't know better, he might have believed her.

She was that fucking good. But his eyes were open to the truth now.

"Is that how you're going to play it?" he asked.

"Play what? It's the truth. I didn't take you for a guy who couldn't handle a girl dumping his ass." Her eyes, rimmed in thick, dark lashes, didn't look away from him. Where was the smiling, sweet girl he'd known? This woman was a hardass.

A roll of his shoulders proved he could be just as insouciant as she. "Nothing to handle. We had a good time. It ended."

"If that's how you feel, then why this?" She gave a wiggle, enough to make the chair creak.

"Because you and I have things to discuss. Such as, whom do you work for?"

"I'm a model. I freelance."

"As a cover. You can drop the act. I know all about you. Marina Francesca Sokolov." Now, at any rate. Before, he'd been a clueless moron who believed every word and every act.

"I see your stalking skills are *en pointe*."

"It's not stalking to find out more about the woman I was sleeping with."

"It is if you do it after she dumps you."

He managed not to flinch or react. She did it on purpose to goad him, and damn her, it was working. "Is it, or is it not, your real fucking name?"

"It's my birth name. I use Francesca Parron for work because my modeling agency recommended it. Now untie me. This is kidnapping and forcible confinement."

"Don't talk to me about laws. I know you break them."

"Says the man who murdered Stefanov." She sniffed and tossed her head.

"I didn't kill him."

"Someone save me. He's crazy," she yelled, struggling against the ropes.

"Drop the act. No one can hear you. And no one will believe those crocodile tears. I know what you really are. What you're capable of."

A cold expression dropped over her features. "Exactly what is it that you think you know?"

"That you're a killer for hire. Go ahead, try and deny it." He knew better. Not as much as he'd like to know, but enough to realize how hard he'd been played.

"Deny what? You've obviously done your homework."

"So you admit to being an assassin?" He'd not wanted to believe it when he heard. Hoped she'd deny it.

She shrugged. "You forgot to mention spy and body-guard. You could say I'm multi-talented."

Fran was talented, all right. She should have mentioned actress. "You're a killer."

Her head tilted, and her lips quirked. "You Americans and your sanctimonious judgment. What I do is no worse than most."

"You kill people."

"Sometimes, for the right sum. I am, after all, a professional. Not some cheap thug hired off the street."

Thing was, Darren didn't have a problem with pros,

or even killing for that matter. Sometimes, it had to be done. What he didn't like was when someone engaged the services of a pro to play *him*.

"Who hired you to seduce me?"

"Who says you were a job?" Her lips quirked.

For a moment, a stupid flutter hit him in the chest —could the connection be real, the fire between them forever? Then he recalled the cold reality.

"Who hired you to spread your legs for me?" He spat it out, still offended by it. As a man who'd sent many a person on a mission, he'd never asked or expected any of his operatives to sleep with anyone.

Francesca flinched. A momentary sign that his words had hit home. Then her lip curled. "I sleep with whomever I want. This isn't the olden days where you can slut-shame me. I had sex with you because you were good-looking."

The praise stroked his ego and only made him madder. "I guess being that close to me made your mission easier."

"It did," she agreed. "But no one paid me to have sex. That was just for fun."

The worst thing was, he knew she'd enjoyed it. He could still remember the ripple of her channel when she orgasmed.

"Who hired you?"

Fran snorted. "Come now, Darren. You and I both know I am not going to answer that."

"You will."

She sighed. "You're being ridiculous."

"There is nothing wrong with demanding answers." He waggled the point of his knife at her.

She still didn't flinch. "Are you going to torture me? Is that what you do now? Torment women because your ego is bruised?"

"The last time I tortured someone, it was with my tongue, and as I recall, you screamed for more."

A slight flare of her nostrils showed that she remembered what he spoke of. There was no mistaking the slight hint of pink in her cheeks. She never could hide her blushes, especially when aroused.

She still wants me, too? Heat flashed through him followed by an instant cold bucket of don't-fall-for-it-you-idiot. This wasn't real.

"You need to let me go. You don't know what you're doing. My surveillance of you was standard industry business. You, of all people, should understand that."

Yes, Darren knew all about espionage, especially that of companies and people. But who was behind it of late? Who kept laying traps and trying to kill the people trained at his academy?

Secundus Academy was a place for those with the right temperament to learn how to be international problem-solving experts. From high-end spying to complex assassinations made to look accidental, the academy trained people who could then go work for independent intelligence agencies or even the government. Secundus prided itself on providing specialized personnel with a wide range of skills. And Darren ran that school. An institution and students someone had been targeting of late.

He leaned forward and captured her gaze. "Since I don't understand, why don't you explain to me what's going on? Why someone is so interested in my movements? Was the same person who hired you to spy on me the one who sent you to the island?" A tropical adventure that ended in tragedy.

"The island is a trap."

"Understatement." Only Darren's staff and a few others had escaped the luxury retreat alive. Many died. Currently, Darren was considered among the dead. A necessary ploy so he could move about unnoticed and hold a woman prisoner without anyone being aware of it.

"Where are we?" She cast a glance around.

He didn't bother. Looking at the luxurious interior of the yacht didn't appeal when he could stare at her. "We're on a boat."

"I can see that," was her sarcastic reply. "Are we docked at the island? If yes, then we have to go. There's a killer here."

"I'd say there's more than one." Both of Darren's bodyguards were pros.

"Would you listen to me? You are in danger so long as you stay on the island."

Why did she care? "Then it's a good thing we left during the storm." The waves at first tossed the yacht up and down, a bobbing toy at the mercy of nature. But it had blown past them, leaving behind calm waters—and churning emotions.

"We're on a boat?"

"Yes. In the middle of the ocean. Which means there's no one to hear you scream."

Her eyes widened. "You won't hurt me."

"Just like you're not the Fran I thought I knew, I'm not the Darren you think, either." A bit of a tongue twister.

"I know you enough to know that you would never cut me open because I won't cooperate. It's not your style."

No, he wouldn't cut her. He wouldn't cross that line. And damn her for knowing that.

So, what could he do to make her talk? He'd do what the academy taught. Find a weakness and exploit it.

With that mantra in mind, he leaned forward and undid the knot holding her wrists.

He set her free.

CHAPTER THREE

HE FREED ME.

Marina Francesca—who adopted each persona depending on circumstance—couldn't believe Darren did it, and at the same time, totally could. The Darren she'd known in Paris wouldn't hurt a woman. Not even one who'd sorely wronged him.

I hurt him. Badly. He could pretend now, but she'd heard how frantically he'd searched for her when she first went missing. He'd initially assumed foul play before he realized she'd left for other reasons.

The job was done.

A mission she almost regretted having taken. But if she had the choice again... She wouldn't hesitate. Marina was a pro, and the assignment had been a simple one. Get close to a specific man. Close enough that she could siphon some information from his phone, his computer, even through conversation, and then, if the right opportunity arose, kill him. Easy money for someone like Marina. Even better, it meant leaving the cold winters of Russia for the warmer climate of France.

She rubbed her wrists and perused his crown of hair as Darren undid her ankle bindings. His hair was still thick and dark with only the occasional gray strand.

Vulnerable as he was, she could kill him right now. He knew it, too, had to, yet he didn't once look up at her as he freed her feet. His body didn't tense. He'd even tucked away the knife.

Fool.

Damn him.

She looked away. "It is a wonder your academy has any graduates who live once they hit the field."

"What academy?"

"Now who's playing stupid? I know all about your precious school full of misfits and bright students with potential." Said with a sneer.

"The academy is a chance for those with specialized skills and a specific mindset to flourish."

"You mean a place for killers to learn."

"We teach them how to do it right. How to avoid getting caught."

"How to make money."

His shoulders rolled. "I won't lie and claim purely altruistic reasons."

"Your school was founded on blood and revenge. Unlike your poor background check of me, I was thorough with you. I know all about your mother's murder. How your father couldn't find justice, so he created his own army of mercenaries. Brilliant, really."

"He saw a need in the world, and he filled it."

"Did he ever find those responsible?" she asked. "Did he hunt them down and paint the world red with their blood? What of those who hired them? Did they suffer, too?" Marina understood revenge.

He didn't reply to her query, choosing to change the subject instead. "Who trained you?"

"I thought you did your homework."

"I got your name and a vague description of a few assignments you might have accomplished. Whoever you work for did a good job wiping your tracks. So, I'll ask you again, who taught you? Was it the DGSE?" The French equivalent of the American CIA.

"Who says my skills aren't natural talent?"

"No one just becomes a mercenary."

"Why not? All you need is the right mindset and a lack of regard for laws."

"That's the definition of a thug. Someone with no finesse, one who makes mistakes and gets caught. You're a pro."

"Thank you." She graciously accepted the compliment before she stood, stretching her limbs, acting casual, wondering if he stared.

He used to love watching me walk naked across the room, his gaze smoldering, his arousal evident. Now, his gaze simmered for another reason.

Would he attack her if she tried to go above deck? He claimed that they were at sea, but for all she knew, they were tethered to a dock with freedom within reach.

"I can see what you're thinking."

"Can you?" She let her lips curve into a teasing

smile. "You thought you knew me in Paris, and we both know how wrong that assumption was."

Judging by the scowl on his face, the reminder didn't please. Darren might not torture or kill her, but she'd be a fool to think he was a pushover. If she threatened, he'd protect himself. Just look at what he'd done so far. Drugged her and taken her prisoner. More than she'd expected. Hotter, too.

"It's not a mistake I'll make again. And you still haven't answered me. Who taught you to be a mercenary? Which agency do you work for?"

"Do you really think I'm going to tell? I'm not an amateur. I would have thought your research on me would have made that clear."

His jaw stiffened. "Declan couldn't get very far with your file. You're well hidden."

"I know."

"Tell me who you are." His frustration boiled over, as evidenced by his shout.

It truly bothered him. So, she made it worse. "I thought we already traded life stories?"

"You mean the fake one you fed me about going to a French boarding school? How your parents didn't pay you any attention?"

"It wasn't completely false." She smiled. "I did go to a private school. But in Russia, not France."

"Russian? I thought you were French."

Her lips tilted into a smirk. "Not even distantly. I would have thought my real name gave it away." Marina Francesca Sokolov. Named after her dead grandmother and some actress her mother admired.

"But your accent..." He frowned. "How come I can't hear any Russian?"

"Because I was taught six languages by the time I was six."

"Six? That's impossible."

"Because Americans mollycoddle their young. In Russia, we don't wait until children are too old to learn. At a young age, recruiters scour the villages and slums, looking for just the right kind of children for their programs."

"How old were you?"

"The youngest they start to take us. Three."

"You were just a baby. How could your parents let you go?"

"It is an honor to be chosen." Usually, it also meant extras for those families. Many of whom were very poor. "At three, I was old enough to dress and care for myself. Old enough to start my lessons."

"Lessons in what?"

She sighed. "Are we really going to waste time going over my academic years one by one, or are you going to ask me what I was doing in Paris?" The last thing she wanted was for him to suddenly soften to her, pity the upbringing she'd endured. The things she'd gone through as a child made her who she was today, but sometimes, she wondered what she'd lost in the process.

"I already asked who hired you, and you said you wouldn't tell. Have you changed your mind?"

"What if I did? What if I said I'd tell you everything I know about Paris?"

"What if I want to find out more about you instead?"

"You can't have both." A woman had to draw a line somewhere, especially when a man made her heart behave erratically. "I'm giving you the choice. Me, or Paris?" Was it strange to hope that he'd ask for the former?

At least Darren didn't immediately reply. Marina could see him at war with himself. Curiosity fighting curiosity. Which question did he most want an answer to?

Eventually, he replied. "What happened in Paris?"

What happened? She'd royally fucked up.

It had seemed like the easiest of missions. Luxurious, too. Given that her agency already had her undercover as a model, her runway shows chosen with an eye on places they needed her to work, she had a decent wardrobe and cover. Her handler arranged for Marina to have a flat. Nothing too spacious—it was Paris, after all, the city of sky-high rents.

But it was hers. Her space. And it didn't have cameras watching her. Her demand because she didn't want to take the chance of her target catching on.

"I never even thought to look for bugs," he muttered, interrupting her narrative.

"Because you fell for me." He could pretend all he wanted, but she knew what had happened.

"I fell victim to your ruse. God, I was so fucking stupid."

No, he was a man in love, but only because he'd been manipulated so deftly. He never stood a chance.

"I was given your image, name, and a bio on you. My mission was to get as close to you as I could."

Marina had met Darren for the first time at an art show. Purposely bumping into him and having him spill his wine on her white dress. Red wine, she might add.

He'd looked utterly horrified, and she'd laughed. Tittered as he offered apology after apology. He didn't stop until she had agreed to go out to dinner with him.

"They had the best hand-rolled gnocchi." She sighed, her turn to stray from the story.

"You threatened to flick a pea at me if I touched them."

She laughed, the remembrance a pleasant one—unlike what happened after. "You looked so shocked. And said—"

"'Like hell are you tossing that pea.' And I reached for a bite of your gnocchi with my fork."

Her lips curved. "So I launched it."

The pea landed in a bowl of soup being carried by a very proper waiter. It splashed, the waiter jumped, the soup sloshed, the cold green crème of asparagus absorbed by an older lady's curly white perm.

They'd left the restaurant laughing and, on the cobblestone street under the light of a Paris moon, shared their first kiss.

His expression softened, and for a moment, they stared at each other, that same electrical awareness stretching between them.

A turn of his head broke the spell, and he barked, "Do you always whore yourself out for your missions?"

A valid question, yet it still hurt. "Do you always attempt to seduce women on a first date?"

"Yes. Luckily, my experience with you didn't stop that."

The implication was clear and hurt when it shouldn't have. Of course he'd slept with other women. He had every right. They were never truly a couple.

She felt a need to hurt him back. "I should hope the fact that I waltzed into your life so easily has made you more cautious now about running background checks."

"I'm always cautious. Whoever set up your background did a great job," he grudgingly admitted.

"But you cracked it?"

"Parts of it. I still haven't figured out where you trained or much else beyond your real name and the fact that you're a killer."

"An operative is only as good as their cover."

"Does this mean you have no life outside of work?"

"I have a life," she retorted. She lived vicariously through her work. "You are getting off topic again. Do you want to hear about Paris or not?"

"What else is there to say? You probably bugged my phone."

"While you showered." She nodded.

"Hacked my computer."

"Not me. But I did use a device to send a mirror copy of your drive to my handler."

He made a sound and shook his head. "I am so fucking stupid. What did they do with that information?"

"Whatever they wanted."

He turned on her, eyes blazing. "What's that supposed to fucking mean?"

"It means, my clients and superiors don't tell me what they do with things, just what they want *me* to do. They say, 'Marina, go get us the grocery list for this person,' and I get it."

"By any means possible."

"Yes." She didn't add that she could have bugged his things quite easily without ever sleeping with him. She'd initially planned to play hard to get. To string him along. But then he'd kissed her, and her panties melted, and she'd forgotten to replace her worn-out vibrator...

He was so much better than a dildo.

So. Much. Better.

She crossed her legs.

"It didn't take you weeks to bug me. Why stick around?"

Because she was also supposed to kill him. Something that appeared accidental. An event that wouldn't look like a hit.

Marina never actually went through with it. Which had cost her a hefty bonus. She blamed it on not finding the right way to do it without leaving a trace. She never acknowledged that it was because she didn't think she could actually kill the man she was sleeping with.

A man who wasn't bad.

A man who took her pleasure very seriously in bed.

A man who looked mad as hell right now, probably because she hadn't replied.

"I said why did you stick around? What else did you do to sabotage me?"

"Apparently, you don't need help doing that. What on earth possessed you to go to the island and put yourself at the mercy of a killer?"

"Careful. You almost sound like you care."

She did not care. He should hope she never cared, or her handler would take care of it.

"Your bodyguards should have never let you come." And was Kacy only his bodyguard? Knowing him as she did, she didn't believe for a moment they were together. Not the way they acted. The man she remembered was always touching. Hand-holding. Stealing nibbles of ears.

At least he had with Francesca in France. But the fake girlfriend he'd brought to the island? He'd barely spared her a glance.

"Marcus tried to talk me out of it, but I'm tired of being dicked around. Someone has been threatening my academy." The school he ran for special operatives like Marina. Except his school didn't start until the kids were teens. No wonder they weren't as good.

"If I were guarding you, I'd have tied you to a bed until you stopped thinking stupid."

"Don't tempt me to hire you." Said in a low growl.

Startled, she looked over at him to see him staring at her. Heat in his gaze. An answering flicker between her legs made her want to scream.

Would it really be that awful to have sex with him one more time? She'd not been satisfied since their last encounter.

"You can't hire me, as I'm still on a mission."

"Not anymore, you aren't. We're no longer on the island."

Which was the one good thing to come out of this situation so far.

"Are there other passengers on the boat?" she asked.

"Doing a head count?" he asked.

"Just making sure you didn't bring the killer with us."

"You know who it is? Who was pulling strings on the island?"

"You don't know yet? It was Gerard." The man who'd greeted them all as they arrived at the island.

"The butler did it?" He said it so comically, she laughed.

"He did, yet I am pretty sure he got his orders from someone else."

"Someone with money. That island and the helicopters that took us in, plus everything else, wouldn't have been cheap."

Indeed, the elaborate plot to lure some of the world's most powerful people, those controlling the mercenary armies, would have cost a fortune.

"Whoever is laying the traps is not worried about the cost," she stated. And where there was money involved, there was always a trail.

"In other words, whoever is targeting my students and me wants a confrontation. The question is, why?"

"Why do people kill?"

"Money, power, or revenge," was his reply. "So, we could be talking about someone whose life was impacted by one of my students' missions."

"It could also be someone who failed your final exams." Francesca shrugged. "Or it could be random.

Your academy and students aren't the only ones being targeted."

"You know for sure it's happening elsewhere, too?" Darren asked sharply. "I've heard rumors."

"I know nothing about rumors, only facts, which is that people have been dying." Some whom she'd known via her work. "It's why Stefanov hired me to accompany him to the island."

"He was your boss?"

"Stefanov was a client," she corrected.

"That makes no sense. I had my guys research him. He supposedly runs his own mercenary company. Why not bring his own team?"

Because most of them were dead. "Staffing issues," was her reply.

"So you were just a lackey."

"I was contracted to protect Stefanov."

"And you talk about my school sucking. You let your client die."

"He was late making payment."

Darren blinked. "Seriously. You let him get murdered because he didn't pay his bill on time?"

"He will serve as a lesson to my next client."

"Was he the one who hired you to spy on me?"

Darren wouldn't stop asking until she replied. "Yes, it was Stefanov. He wanted intelligence on the competition."

He glowered. "Is he the one who's been going after the Bad Boy agents?"

"How would I know? As you said, I was just a lackey."

"If you had to guess?"

Did he seriously just ask her opinion? She almost laughed. "Do I think Stefanov was risking a war with the other mercenary groups around the world? No. He's not that dumb, but I do think he might have been hired or coerced into doing things."

"What makes you say that?"

"Because he made some stupid decisions. As a result, many of his crew died. One of them was killed recently by someone in your Bad Boy crew."

"Bad Boy is not mine," he interrupted.

"So you say and yet they often perform missions for you."

"Because I pay them."

At a discount. "Whatever," she replied with a shrug. "You wanted to know about Stefanov. He was hired to mess with Bad Boy. He said something about a drug ring…"

"That was one of his men?" Darren swore. "Fucker. My agents almost died because of that bastard."

"Then you've been lucky. There are many operatives whose ashes now feed the snow fields." Being a soldier in a hidden army wasn't a long-term career choice for many. Although, if you did make it past forty, chances were you'd earned a comfy position with an office and a salary for life.

"How do I know that what you're telling me now is the truth? Why should I believe anything you say?"

"Don't." She shrugged. "You asked me questions. I'm giving answers."

"And conveniently blaming everything on a dead man."

"Not everything. I did say I thought someone else was controlling him."

"But who?"

"That is your problem."

'Shouldn't you make it yours, too?"

"Until they come directly for me...no. I see no reason to go on a personal quest. Especially if there is no money involved." She already had enough on her plate without taking on a new vendetta.

"What about the fact that people are losing their lives?"

"It is the circle of life."

"That's cold."

"It's reality," she said. She tested him by pacing to the far end of the cabin. The boat rocked gently under her feet. She wondered if there was anyone aboard helping him sail. Or were they currently bobbing adrift at sea? The very thought made her want to find a life vest.

"What other missions have you done for Stefanov? Other than spying on me."

"I was supposed to kill you."

"In Paris?"

"Yes. But that fell through." She didn't mention the part about her conscience forestalling the killing blow. She wouldn't want him to think she was soft. She'd had enough dealing with the harangue from Sergei—her handler—about her incompetence.

His jaw went taut. "You would have killed me? How?

In bed, while I was sleeping? Just slit my throat? Or would you have gone for something more impersonal like a bullet to the head?"

"Paris was supposed to look like an accident."

"Why did Stefanov want me dead?"

"I don't know."

"You were just going to kill a man without reason?"

"If the money is right. And even if it wasn't, those were my orders."

"Do you ever question your directives?"

"Do your operatives?"

To her surprise, he said, "Yes. Actually, they do. And if their reason is valid, we listen."

"We?" she parroted with an arch of her brow. "I thought Bad Boy wasn't yours."

"Graduating from the academy doesn't mean I abandon the students. I stay in contact with the places they're hired by. Some more closely than others. I make sure the people the academy trains aren't being abused."

"And if they are?"

"I'd step in and say something."

"Must be nice. You grew up in a land where you can speak your mind. You can say whatever you like. Not everyone has that choice." The Americans complained about their freedom, never realizing that being allowed to complain was the biggest freedom of all. They should step into other worlds to grasp what they took for granted.

"There is such a thing as defection."

She paused, her fingers pressed against the porthole window in the wall, the vista of blue reaching as far as she could see. She stared over her shoulder at him. "You think I should abandon my country and everything I know to...what? Become a spy for the other side?"

"Why not?"

"Loyalty to my country, for one."

"Your country sucks."

At that, she stood tall and thrust her shoulders back. "I will have you know that Russia is the best country in the world."

"A country that allowed you to be taken as a small child and stuck in a boot camp."

"For which I am grateful. Without their intervention, I would have gone to regular school and probably ended up in a factory. Instead, I get to wear beautiful clothes, travel the world. Eat fine food, and drink expensive wine."

"Sleep with men for information. Kill them."

"You say that like those are bad things." She smiled. "Some people deserve to die."

"Do I?"

"Only if you touch my gnocchi." The light retort saw his expressions fighting themselves, the softness warring with the anger.

"Keep making jokes. We'll stay out at sea until you tell me everything I want to know."

"You can't do that. You must take me to shore."

"When you tell me everything, and I've verified it."

"And what if I don't know the answers?"

"You'd better hope you do."

She flattened her lips. "I don't have time for your games. I must report in."

"They think you're dead."

"I can tell you right now, they know I'm alive. The longer I don't report in, the worse it will be."

"Then don't report back in ever again. You tell me what I want to know, and I'll have the boat deposit you somewhere where you can start over."

If only it were that simple. "You idiot. Listen to me. I can't start over, nor can I stay here with you. I'm being tracked. As in, somewhere in my body, there's a chip transmitting my location."

"Your agency chips its operatives?"

"Doesn't yours?"

Darren struggled before he bit out, "Yes, but we would never use it against them. We only use the trackers in case the agents go missing and are in need of rescue."

"You mean if they've been kidnapped?" was her sarcastic retort. "My handler will use the chip to find me. If you are still alive when they do, then I will be punished for being negligent. Unless I am somehow incapacitated." Her expression brightened as she got an idea. She sat in the chair and laced her hands behind her back. "Tie me up."

"What? No."

"Yes, tie me up. That way, when they find me, I will have an excuse for not killing you."

"You want me to tie you up so you don't have to kill me?" he said it slowly.

"Yes."

"Why don't you want to kill me?"

Her excuse had nothing to do with any mission and

everything to do with her wet panties. "Because the sex was good. And the world is small. Maybe we'll find the time to have sex again one day."

It should have been the perfect carrot to dangle, the opening to have him kissing her instead of asking endless questions. It didn't work as expected.

Darren stalked out of the cabin, leaving her yelling, "Come back here and tie me up!"

Alas. He left her free.

CHAPTER FOUR

TIE ME UP.

Was she fucking insane?

No, apparently, she was Russian, which made her even more unpredictable. It also made her entire story suspect. How much of what she said was actually the truth? How much was fiction?

Darren pondered it as he took the steps to the upper deck of the yacht two at a time. The salty air hit his skin, and he breathed deeply, trying to clear the turmoil in his head—and his damned heart.

He shouldn't have felt a damned thing for her. He thought himself past hurt and anger. Wrong. Just like he'd wrongly thought himself over her. The moment he saw her, all the old feelings, the good ones, rushed back. The temptation she posed proved as strong as ever, despite what she'd done and in spite of who she was.

I hate that I still want her.

He lifted his face to the sky. The dawning sun

beamed over the horizon, baking him with its brilliance. Stripping away most of the shadows that clung to him. Some stubbornly refused to melt away.

Don't forgive her. Remember what she did. Fran had used him to complete a mission. He'd fallen for a lie. Hurt for something that never truly existed.

What did that make him?

Stupid. So moronic, he couldn't even follow through on his plan to torture her. Nope, dumbass that he was, he'd set her free. He'd probably end up dead because he was soft. Did she, at this very moment, seek out a weapon to kill him?

She could probably kill me with her bare hands. If she touched him, he'd probably let her. She had such deft fingers. Perfect digits to wrap around his cock and stroke.

His body turned traitor, especially one particular part, as it remembered the past.

He gripped the rail and leaned over, looking at the still waters reflecting the colorful dawn. The ocean was much calmer this morning. Still enough that he'd shut down the engines and dropped anchor in the middle of nowhere.

Nowhere to escape. Nowhere to hide.

Yet, Fran seemed to think someone could track them. She really didn't give him any credit. Little did she know that he had something on board to block electronic signals. He wasn't an amateur. His boat had all the newest gadgets and toys, and an invisible pilot to help. Which meant, he could be out here alone with her.

Help isn't coming, Fran. But he'd let her think it might be for a while longer.

Darren heard the whisper of steps. He didn't turn, playing the hapless victim for a woman who'd admitted to her Russian spy upbringing and killer nature.

A woman who couldn't bring herself to eliminate me, not in Paris or on the rooftop patio on the island.

For some reason, he kept returning to that one glaring fact. She could have murdered him, many times over. Could have, but instead, she'd allowed him to take her prisoner.

Why? That was the one thing he couldn't figure out. Killers didn't get cold feet. They couldn't hesitate or show mercy because they never knew if the one that got away would be the one to put a bullet between their eyes.

A knife didn't materialize between his shoulders blades, and he didn't get shoved into the big blue sea. She let him live, which meant she wanted something from him.

Does she want me? He really had to stop with the foolish flights of fancy.

Darren turned to face her. She looked fetching despite her disheveled appearance, her clothes wilted from the rain they'd encountered on the way to the yacht. Navigating the floating dock with her over a shoulder as it heaved with each angry swell had proven interesting.

"This is a nice ship," she remarked. "Yours?"

"Yes. I managed to get a message out." When people started dying, he'd decided it was time to get himself and his team off that island. The boat had arrived and docked as the storm hit. Darren ended up boarding it without his team. He left them to clean up the mess so he could deal with Fran on his own.

"Is that the coast?" She pointed at a dark line on the horizon.

"Yes. You going to swim for it?"

"Would you let me?"

"I would, but I feel like I should mention that there are sharks in these waters." He stared pointedly at her.

She rolled her eyes. "Are you really going to whine about my job again? Kind of hypocritical since your school provides the same kind of training."

"We're not the same." He heard the defensive, angry note in his statement.

"We are. My being Russian doesn't make it any better or worse. We just work for opposing sides. Why not admit that the real reason you're upset is because you never once caught on?"

He hadn't. How could he have been so blind? "I'm not upset."

"Liar. Anyone can see you are bothered by the fact I'm an agent. Or is it because you were bested by a woman?"

"That's where you're wrong. The women I know have always been more dangerous than the men."

"Then why act so offended?"

"If I were offended, would I offer you a job? Work for me." Darren had not even known he'd say it until the offer spilled from his lips.

He could see he'd taken her off guard. "I am not defecting."

"I never said defect. I said work for me. That is what you do, right? Take jobs for rich clients. Or do you only work for Russian employers?"

"Nationality is not a problem." He could see he'd piqued her curiosity when she asked, "A job doing what?"

"I need a new bodyguard."

That truly dropped her jaw. "Me? Why? You have your man, Marcus."

A giant meathead who'd worked for him for years and was now a friend. "I think Marcus might be asking for time off soon." He'd met a girl. About time.

"So you think it's a good idea to ask a Russian spy—one who's been told to kill you—to protect you instead? Are you high?"

"No, I'm practical. Come work for me. I'll make it worth your while."

"I can't."

"Why not? I'll pay you."

"That's just it. I'm not an independent contractor. Everything has to go through my superiors."

"Fine. Call them and tell them I want to hire you."

"No." She shook her head. "You're just trying to fool me."

"Fool you how? You keep assuming you know me and what I'm going to do."

"I do know you."

"Because of Paris? Who says the Darren you met in Paris is the real me?" That person had died. This man was older and wilier, but obviously not wiser. Only an idiot would hire an assassin from the other side.

She shook her head. "My superiors will never go for it."

"Why don't you try asking first?"

"You aren't going to stop until I say yes, are you?" she said with a sigh.

"I'm a man who gets what he wants." Except with her.

"I'll need to make a call before I can give you an answer."

He knew she expected him to balk. Which was why he pulled out a burner phone he had placed on board. The real reason he was in sight of the coast? Just enough signal to get a call out to the mainland.

She eyed him then the phone. "This is crazy."

Yes. And it felt great. Darren was usually the responsible academy owner. Pushing paper. Ensuring he kept the funding at the right levels, brought in the right kind of specialists to teach. He didn't have much to do with the students or their missions once they left his training grounds. It just looked like he had close ties with Bad Boy because of his friendship with Harry who fed him stories secondhand. Only recently had he gotten to live an adventure and have some fun. He wasn't ready to go back to the office and push more paper.

Francesca dialed a number and held the phone to her ear. When she spoke in a rapid-fire stream of Russian, it took him by surprise. Surely, he'd not expected otherwise? Yet it did shock him because he'd heard her speak flawless French, and her English had only a hint of an accent. Now, she showed her linguistic skills with yet another language. The musical beauty of the speech, even if barked at times, captivated him.

What did she say? Had he grossly miscalculated? Was she even now planning her extraction and his demise?

He blinked as her words, in English, penetrated. "Sergei is asking how much you are willing to pay."

"For what?"

"What do you think? The job."

Ah, yes. His spur-of-the-moment offer for her to work for him. Because he was fucking insane. However, he couldn't back out. Not now. Maybe if he under-quoted, they'd say no and let him off the hook.

"Five thousand a day." The ridiculous sum, five times what he paid Marcus, slipped off his tongue.

She blinked. She spat something in Russian at the phone. Then stared at him. Someone replied. "Sergei says for that price you can have three more agents."

"No, I just want you." How true that claim resonated.

She nattered again in Russian. Asked him a few more questions—How long? What kind of danger was expected? Duties? He didn't say *bedroom activities*, but he wondered if Sergei did when her brow creased and she barked into the phone.

A frown on her face, she hung up and handed it back. "Congratulations, I now work for you."

Someone didn't sound happy. So he just had to push it. "Sir."

"Excuse me?"

"As your boss, shouldn't you address me as sir?"

He was pretty sure the stream of language coming from her mouth didn't have the word *sir* in it. He waited until she was done to grind her a bit more. "Are we going to have an issue, or are you capable of being a pro?"

Fran struggled with her scowl. "You bought me and now expect me to be your lap dog."

"As you keep reminding me, this is what you do. I'd think you'd be happy. I'm an easy job. Real easy to please." Giving her pleasure was what he truly enjoyed.

"I won't sleep with you."

"What if someone attacks me while I'm asleep? That happened you know, a few days before my house got blown up." An unfortunate accident that had happened during an assassination attempt.

"I heard. You need to upgrade your security."

"And that's why we should share a room." He pushed her a little harder.

"I will be close by."

"You'll have to be more than close at the end of the month."

"Why?"

"Wedding. I'll need you to come as my plus one."

"Expecting trouble?"

"Only if we're lucky. It's a hitman wedding for one of our best students, Reaper."

"He's still alive?" She looked impressed.

"You know him?"

"Not personally, but he has been used as an example of not being stupid and living a long, fruitful life."

It irritated Darren to no end that she found Reaper interesting. "He's getting married. For real. And we're throwing a big party. Inviting everyone to it."

"I take it you don't like him," she stated.

"Of course I like him, or I wouldn't have offered to pay for the damned thing."

"You like him so much that you would paint a target on him by throwing a large wedding? Is it his friends you hate?"

"Nope. A lot of them are acquaintances of mine, too."

"It's a trap," she finally stated.

"Exactly. We're counting on drawing the wrong kind of attention. It's going to be the biggest mercenary bash ever thrown, and all the bad guys are invited."

Her lips quirked. "Don't forget the bad girls."

"Wouldn't be a party without them. So, you'll be my date?"

"As my employer, you'll be required to dress me for the occasion."

"Of course."

"I need a weapon."

"I'll make sure you have the very best."

"Not then. Now."

"What do you mean now?"

She pointed behind him.

He turned to see, wondering if this was when she'd make her move and toss him overboard. Except he realized the distant whup-whup-whup sound was a pair of helicopters, and they were coming toward them.

Didn't mean shit. They were in waters close to the Keys. Helicopters flew around all over the place. Tourists wanting to see the whales and dolphins. People jumping between the islands. This was an everyday occurrence and nothing to panic about.

Not according to his new bodyguard.

Fran planted her hands on her hips and snapped, "Stop staring like that idiot Ivan who got run over by the tank and show me the weapons cabinet."

"How does someone get run over by a tank?"

"By being stupid. Like you right now. Where do you keep the guns?"

"Below deck in a locked cabinet."

"Perfect. After you open it for me, you will find yourself a corner to hide in." Fran turned into a dominant force of nature and ordered him around.

Not happening. "I am not hiding."

"As your new bodyguard, I say you are."

"I'm your boss, and I'm telling you no."

She glared. "It is going in my report to Sergei that you are a difficult client."

"For refusing to act cowardly?"

"Refusing a direct protective order, thereby placing your life at risk, which means I must put *my* life at risk. There is an extra fee for each occurrence."

"You're going to charge me extra for being assertive?"

"No, we are charging you more for being stupid," she corrected, following him below deck.

As he dialed the combination for the safe, she kept craning to peer out the door.

"Hurry up, they are moving in fast."

"Doesn't mean it's for us," he said.

"Seems awfully coincidental given that there's nothing around us."

"If they're homing in on our location, then it's because of your phone call." He paused, leaning against the gun cabinet. "Did you call for help and lie about it?"

She frowned. "Why would I lie? I don't need help." She lunged, wrapping an arm around him, jabbing her fingers into his skin, sapping his strength. "I can take care of myself, and you."

She kept pressing, and he went limp. Too late to curse his own stupidity. The problem with letting his dick and emotions rule him. His eyes shut before he hit the floor.

CHAPTER FIVE

EVEN THE BIGGEST MEN COULDN'T FIGHT BIOLOGY—or pressure points. Darren succumbed, his heavy body slumping as gravity dragged it to the floor. Right in her way, of course. Given his big frame blocked the door of the weapons cabinet, Francesca had to shove him out of the way. Being a smart operative, she'd waited for the click of the safe lock indicating he'd opened it before she took him out—for his own protection.

Darren might have some field skills, but he was a white-collar, operations type who worked with paper and handshakes, not in the field where every decision counted. He lacked experience and know-how. This, however, was what she did. Protect the client. Sergei had been very clear. Even without the money, her orders were to keep Darren alive until further notice. Especially since he might know more about who pulled the strings on the island.

While not well liked, Stefanov remained a person of

import. The fact that he'd been killed wouldn't sit well. It didn't help that many would wonder if they might be killed next. If a man like Stefanov could fall, then who was safe?

Whoever hunted them on that island was not only well-informed but also well-armed. Just look at the approaching helicopters. Overkill to sink one little boat with two people aboard.

Was someone peeved that Darren had escaped the island and the murder game they'd tried to play? Too bad. When it came to games, Marina didn't like to lose.

Grabbing a rifle from the cabinet, as well as tucking Darren's knife into a pocket, she moved to the doorway leading to the deck, the whupping beat of rotor blades loud. She dared a peek, squinting against the dawning light, and noted the choppers getting close but still high overhead. She couldn't see any markings on them. They were still too far out. But coming in fast.

An exit onto the deck, and the whipping winds caught at her hair. She held the rifle behind her back and used her free hand to cover her eyes against the glare of the sun as she stared at the incoming helicopters.

According to Darren, they could be benign. Her gut said otherwise.

One of them veered off to the left, while the other kept coming.

Closer.

Closer. Dipping low so that it just skimmed the tops of the water.

Closer still. Almost on top of them.

She didn't loosen her grip on the gun, nor did she stop watching.

Perhaps this was just someone gawking, but instinct had been honed into her from a young age. She knew better than to ignore it. When her gut yelled, *Move!* she dove sideways and heard the *pop-pop-pop* and thud of bullets smacking into the wooden planks.

I was right. She couldn't wait to rub it in Darren's face because she had every intention of surviving to taunt him.

She ducked around the side of the wheelhouse, brought the rifle to her shoulder, counted to three, and heaved in a big breath. Leaning out, she raised the rifle and sighted almost blindly.

Bang. Bang. Bang.

The windshield of the chopper cracked from the bullet that hit it. A ping said another shot ricocheted, while the third appeared to have missed.

Her shooting instructor would have yelled at her for such crappy aim.

She ducked back behind the wheelhouse, turning her face to the side as a spray of bullets splintered the deck. Despite not being a nautically minded person, she knew the boat couldn't accept much abuse or they'd start taking on water. The battle needed to end now before it was too late, but how to fight against a chopper that even now wheeled about for another run? A pity there wasn't a rocket launcher in the gun cabinet.

If Sergei had planned this, I'd have a rocket launcher and more.

The boat engine suddenly came to life, a growl to

counter the whir of the helicopter blades. Was there someone else on board? She'd never had a chance to check.

A peek upward showed no one driving the ship, yet the anchor was lifting, the rattle of chain automated and startling.

She popped out to shoot again at the helicopter, most of her shots missing but for one. The money shot. She must have hit the pilot because the chopper listed, dipping forward, coming toward the boat. *Zaebis!*

More Russian curse words might have erupted except the boat lurched, throwing her off balance. She spread her arms, just barely bracing against the wheel-house as the boat moved out of the path of the crashing helicopter.

One of the revolving blades screamed along the metal railing as the aircraft tipped into the ocean with a big splash. Water sloshed over the deck of the yacht, soaking her feet. Marina ran across to the other side of the boat and got to see the commotion underwater as the chopper kept sinking, the blades still churning until the engine died. What didn't die so easily was the shooter.

A head bobbed up in the ocean water swells.

Don't show mercy. To hesitate is to invite your own death. A lesson she never forgot.

She lifted the rifle and fired. The waves messed with her shot, heaving the target so that his shoulder, not his head, blossomed red. Not a killing wound, but spilling enough blood to ensure that he wouldn't be rescued, not in these hungry waters.

One danger taken care of, she took a breath and wondered again at the mobility of the yacht. The ghost-driven boat kept chugging, and a peek downstairs showed Darren still passed out. She clambered into the wheelhouse and was disturbed to see the steering wheel moving without aid. A crackling of the radio. "Big Kahuna, Big Kahuna, this is Fraggle Q. Do you read? We're showing impact."

She grabbed the receiver and clicked it. "Are you driving the boat?"

A surprised voice barked, "Who the fuck is this? What have you done with the boss man?"

"He's fine, but not for long." Because if she weren't mistaken, she heard a new whup-whup from the other helicopter, the one that had veered away. It was coming at her from a different direction. Playing chase.

"Where's the boss? I want to talk to him."

"Darren can't come to the phone right now, and we're in trouble. Bogey coming in hot." She'd watched the movies. For some reason, speaking the slang put men at ease.

"Motor doesn't have much more to give. I'll see what I can do." The engine on the yacht screamed as it throttled harder, racing for shore. Who was this guy controlling the damned boat? Did it matter? At least he was trying to get them away from the helicopter.

A peek over her shoulder through the window showed it wasn't close to enough. "Unless you've got a missile launcher on the rear end of this thing, it's not enough."

"I'll send—"

She cut him off. "There's no time." Taking down one helicopter was impressive enough. Taking down a second with limited resources? They needed a miracle. Or a bigger gun. Maybe she'd not seen all the available weaponry. Did this thing have a hidden gun? None of the blinking lights screamed, *Slap me for a super-secret machine gun turret*. Pity.

The helicopter neared. She'd run out of time.

She took the stairs two at a time, thumping hard, momentarily losing sight of the chopper. She ducked below deck as it showed off its firepower, the heavy artillery smashing into the deck, splintering the wooden boards, causing epic destruction. Oddly enough, nothing hit the cabin.

Boom. Something exploded at the back of the yacht, and it shuddered, a body-jarring heave and groan of bending metal. Even worse, the motor coughed.

Things were about to get bad. As in sunken-ship bad.

This was a first for her. She'd have to tell Sergei to add it to the bill. Because she had no intention of drowning today. Nor did she intend to let Darren die. Her mission was to keep him alive.

She dove below deck, avoiding the strafing gunfire. She scrounged in the first cupboard she saw, then another, until she found some life jackets, the vest kind that inflated with the pull of a cord. She wedged one over Darren's head, contrary to the instructions on airplanes, and then put one on herself. She quickly cinched them both, trying to ignore the fact that the boat engine had died. They slowed to a stop.

Quack. They sat dead in the water, an easier target than a sitting duck, and those attacking in the chopper knew it. They fired lazily now. Just enough to keep her from popping out.

As she strapped Darren's waist strap for his vest, she thought furiously.

If we go out the door, they'll shoot us. But staying inside, we'll drown.

However, there were worse things than a lungful of water. More painful ways to die.

The acrid stench of smoke reached her. A fire, perhaps started by the dead engine, not that the how mattered. A fire on board would burn without a care. If the smoke didn't get them first.

She stuck her head out of the hatch for a peek, only to quickly pull back when a spraying splinter narrowly missed her cheek.

No exit that way. The windows were too small.

She went scrounging some more, trying not to give in to panic as water inched into the cabin, quickly covering her feet. Then swirling around her ankles. Those bastards, they'd put a hole in the boat.

She propped Darren up, now cursing the fact that she'd knocked him out. She could have used his knowledge of the tools on board. She leaned him against a banquette and then shoved him to the side to look inside the storage area of the seat.

What she found made her smile.

It would be a long shot. If she failed, they'd drown for sure. But as her *uchitel*—her teacher—used to say, "If you're afraid of wolves, don't go in to the woods unless you have a gun." Which had no bearing on this situation, much like every single expression her teacher had spouted.

But in times like these, remembering them helped to center her. She filched the rope Darren had used on her earlier. When the water hit their knees, she inflated the vests. The rope had two purposes. One to lash him to the floatation device she found. Then, she tethered the loose end around her waist. The water kept rising, and rather than give in to panic, she took deep breaths. She gripped the device she'd found as the water hit her chest.

The gunfire appeared to have stopped, but she still heard the helicopter hovering overhead, waiting to see if the job was done.

It wouldn't be long now. The boat was sinking. The life jacket did its job, floating her, lifting her feet off the floor. At her back, Darren bobbed, flotsam that couldn't escape her because of the rope.

Rope is good when it's long; speech is good when it's short. The voice in her head again sounded like Kristoff, her teacher, his guttural words of wisdom a daily occurrence as she grew up. He'd finally retired last year to a place in the country with chickens and a small garden plot. His potato vodka was very good.

As the water neared the ceiling, she knew it was time. They had only inches left. One last glance at Darren. She hoped her plan would work, or they'd be feeding the fish—and making them fat.

She turned on the switch for the sea scooter, hoping

against hope that, on a ship this modern, it would be charged before being put away.

It whirred to life and instantly yanked her forward. She aimed it for the door, holding her breath, hoping Darren didn't swallow too much seawater, and off they went.

The sea scooter leading the way, they shot out of the doorway into the cresting daylight, a torpedo that lagged because of the flotsam she dragged.

She didn't escape unnoticed. *Rat-tat-tat*. Bullets peppered the water.

None hit her, and she could only hope her unconscious luggage remained unharmed—and didn't start screaming. She'd lose all respect for him if he did.

She whipped them around, sending the Darrenfloaty at her back swinging, the rope tugging on her waist digging into flesh. She kept her grip on the scooter, barely, and held on as they shot in the opposite direction. It wouldn't fool the chopper for long. It would spin around and give chase. She'd bought them very little time.

Which meant she needed a plan.

She eyed the dark line of shore. Civilization. And people watching. Would the helicopter dare attack in front of an audience?

They'd soon find out.

Now we race. She held the throttle down as far as it would go and arrowed for land.

CHAPTER SIX

THE WATER SPLASHING HIS FACE MADE HIM SPUTTER, gasp, then gurgle as his open mouth took in more liquid. Saltwater. Gag.

What the fuck! Darren blinked open his eyes and stared at a bright blue—

"Aaaah!" Suddenly airborne, he couldn't help but yell, a sound cut short as he hit hard. Water sprayed. In that moment, he realized a few things.

One, he was still at sea, no longer on his boat but tied to a freaking life preserver, whipping across waves.

Two, the drunken racing was to evade the fucking helicopter chasing them. From his vantage point, he saw the guns fire and miss him, barely.

And three. "You're fucking nuts!" Did Fran seriously think they could outrun a helicopter with a sea scooter? Which made him wonder where his pretty boat had gone.

Rat-tat-tat. More bullets peppered the water and

only missed him because she veered hard enough to send him whipping in a different direction, screwing with the shot. This time. Eventually, one of those bullets would lodge in his body and hurt. He really wanted to avoid that; however, his options were rather limited at the moment.

Since looking at the helicopter made him antsy, the next time he went airborne, he managed a flip, landing stomach down, which meant a face full of water. He plowed through the waves, eyes shut, mouth shut, barely able to get a breath.

He flipped back to his fucked turtle position and yelled again. "You're going to kill us."

"Not dead yet," she hollered back, whipping them into another circle.

Yet being the keyword. It wouldn't be long. The chopper might be having a hard time aiming at them, but they'd eventually get lucky despite her erratic weaving.

So imagine his surprise when the chopper veered off.

Fran, however, didn't slow their pace.

"Would you fucking stop? They're gone."

"Not safe," was her reply.

When she did finally slow enough that he could breathe without fearing a mouthful of water, he immediately flipped to his belly and got to glare at her back.

"What the hell is wrong with you?"

"You're welcome."

"For what?"

"Saving your life."

She had, yet at the same time... "You almost killed me. Untie me before you fucking drown me."

"So ungrateful. Fear not, Sergei will ensure that you show proper gratitude when you pay your bill." She kept one hand on the scooter as she turned with a knife in the other.

He showed no fear as the blade came toward him. She wouldn't go through this much trouble to kill him now.

The rope holding him to the life preserver severed suddenly, and he rolled off it but kept a hold by slapping an arm on the floating boogie board. "Care to tell me what the hell happened?"

"The helicopters sank your pretty boat. I saved us."

"I wouldn't have needed saving if you hadn't attacked me."

"Because you wouldn't obey."

"And you thought knocking me out was a better plan?"

"Yes. After all it worked for you when you did it to me."

The reminder made him glare. "Knocking me out was revenge?"

"No. I did it so I could do my job. You know, the one you hired me for. Protecting your delicate butt."

"My ass isn't delicate. I'm capable of taking care of myself."

"No, you're not, or you wouldn't have argued with me about those choppers."

"You were right. Happy? And I would add that the

only reason we're even arguing is because that chopper let us go."

"This isn't an argument, it's a lively discussion. And the reason it let us go is because of my brilliance. You can thank me for being alive."

"We're adrift at sea."

"Not quite. There is the shore." She pointed, and he looked at the dark band of land.

"It's pretty far. What if that chopper comes back?" Or his enemies sent a boat. They were utterly screwed.

"What if, what if. We don't whine about what-ifs in Russia."

"Well, maybe you should. We're far from safe." A fact reinforced when he noticed a fin pop up about a dozen or so yards from them. "Um, Fran, we should really get going. Looks like we have company. We still got some juice in that thing?"

"Some. It was not happy lugging your heavy carcass."

"Heavy? I'm very trim."

"For a man your age."

He scowled. "Did you just call me old?"

"You complain like an old man."

Funny how the longer they bickered, the more he noticed a slight accent. As if a layer of fake peeled away.

"This old man doesn't want to drown or get eaten by sharks."

"Bah, they will eat me first. I am the one bleeding." She held up her arm, and sure enough, a line of red streaked down, which explained the second fin that appeared.

"Let's go." He grabbed hold of the sea scooter, planning to wrench it from her grip.

She held tight. "I will drive."

"Like hell. The first time, you almost killed me."

"If I'd killed you, you'd be talking less."

He growled.

She smiled. Then let go suddenly. "Very well, you drive. I will protect us." She waved the knife in her hand.

"Try not to cut me with that thing," he grumbled as she slid her arms around his waist.

"I am not an amateur. If I cut, it will be on purpose," she promised.

He grabbed the handles and squeezed the lever. The scooter shot forward, distracting him from the fact that she was holding on, her body wrapped around his. As they sped through the water, he kept a sharp eye out for sharks, speedboats, hell, anything at this point. He couldn't believe the brazenness of someone coming after them in broad daylight, guns blazing.

What happened to subtle?

The shoreline neared, and—staggered out from it—reefs and rocky shoals they'd have to avoid, but that also hid them for the moment. He aimed for the nearest one, especially given the motor was starting to lag, and they slowed in the water. Slowed right down to the point he might have swum faster, and still, the shoal wasn't quite within reach.

Something brushed by his leg.

Don't look down. Don't look down.

He looked down. Saw the cigar shape of a shark swimming under him. Not good.

"We're going to have to swim the rest of the way," he announced as the motor died a little more, barely chugging them across the water.

"Okay." She slid off him and began to stroke for the coral. He gaped, especially since he saw the fin trailing after her.

"Fran. Fuck. Behind you." A part of him worried yelling would distract her, but he couldn't do or say nothing with a predator practically nipping at her toes.

So, what did his crazy ex-French ex-girlfriend-now-turned-Russian-spy do? She stopped swimming, treaded water, and when the fin bumped a little too close? She went sushi chef on its ass.

The gore of shark blood clouded the water, the maimed fish sinking, acting as a lodestone to the predators in the area. When she was done, she put the knife between her teeth and began swimming anew as if she fought off sharks every day.

Hell, for all he knew, she did.

She peered back at him. "Swim faster."

He didn't need her urging to get his ass in gear. "Don't worry about me," he huffed as he stroked, keeping his head above water.

"You're slow," she snapped as she treaded water, knife in hand, gaze staring below her. "In Russia, we swam five miles every morning. The slowest person didn't get breakfast. Sometimes, I lost on purpose to ensure I wouldn't get fat. You, on the other hand, have obviously not been earning your meals."

The goading worked. He put his head down and stroked, pulling hard in the water, trying not to think what might be eyeing him as a tasty snack. He only slowed when his hand slapped smoothed rock. He bobbed in the water alongside Fran, ignoring the churn behind them.

He heaved himself onto the shoal, careful of the sharper edges. He even tucked his feet up on it as Fran joined him. Behind, there was still a swarm of fins. In the distance, he could see the black speck of a chopper, possibly going out to investigate what had happened. Or was it looking for them?

Either way, they couldn't stay here. Darren peeked over at the land, an island teeming with bodies.

Naked bodies.

No way could they make it amongst them without notice.

Fran must have realized it, too. "We will stick out like a black eye on a pretty woman."

"We have to do something. We can't sit out here in the sun all day."

"Wait like cowards?" She snorted. "Never. I have a plan."

"Why do I get the impression I won't like it?"

"Because you are ashamed of the human body. I, on the other hand, am not." With that declaration, she stripped out of her lifejacket and clothes.

He might have gaped. Sure, he'd seen her body naked before. Licked just about every inch of it, too, but it had been a while. He might have ogled, which was why he probably didn't react quickly enough when she came at him with her knife.

She used it deftly. Without mercy.

He had no defense.

In no time at all, he was naked, too.

He glared at her. "Did you have to do that?"

"Now we fit in. Come on. Let's get to the beach before the next attackers come after us."

"They wouldn't dare. Not in front of a crowd." He'd wager that was why the helicopter had turned away.

"Stop arguing with me." She stood on the rock, tall, lean, and proud.

He scrambled to his feet to prevent her looming over him. She smiled.

Then shoved him off the reef.

CHAPTER SEVEN

THE NUDE BEACH PROVED ENTERTAINING—FOR Marina.

Not everyone had as much fun. Darren still scowled. Apparently, he didn't appreciate how she'd rescued him. He grumbled things about loss of dignity and how his ass hurt because of the pinching.

He should thank her. It could have been worse if the ladies—and men—on the beach thought he was available. By placing her mark on him, she'd made him off limits.

But did he thank her for the admiration of his posterior? Nope. He complained she'd left a bruise. Utterly ungrateful. She'd be sure to tell Sergei. There was a billing code for that, as well.

His litany of grumbles didn't stop there. He protested about the clothes she stole as if she'd purposely chosen the one locker with the tight shorts and skimpy tank top for him—she had, actually—for personal entertainment.

"I look like a gigolo," he complained, sitting beside her in the taxi they'd managed to flag. She'd stolen some cash from the locker, too. And a phone. She had to make some calls.

"You look like a proper vacationer."

"An indecent one." He kept his folded hands on his lap, hiding the outline of his man parts. Impressive bits, she should add.

"Would you have preferred to remain in the water until nightfall?" she asked.

"I would have liked to keep my clothes."

"We needed to blend in." Not that Darren truly did with his superb body and proud bearing. He drew too many gazes.

"We could have swum farther down the beach."

"It was too risky to stay in the water. Stop being such a prude."

"Don't mock me. I don't like being nude in public."

Her turn to tease. "But you didn't mind doing other things." When they got together, the passion tended to overwhelm propriety.

His lips flattened, and his hands shifted in his lap. "Momentary lapse of reason."

She hid a smile. "If you say so."

"Where are we going?" he asked, pretending interest in the scenery flashing by outside. They were still somewhere in the Keys, a string of islands at the southern tip of Florida linked by numerous bridges.

"We are going to a safe place."

"Which tells me nothing."

"Exactly."

"Pass me the phone." He held out his hand.

"Why?"

"I should probably call Marcus and let him know I'm alive."

"No. You'll call no one." She flicked a glance at the driver whose head bopped up and down, his wireless earbuds blasting some tunes. She turned her gaze back to Darren. "For now, whoever sent those helicopters after you, thinks you're dead."

"You think the island mastermind is the one behind today's attack?"

"That seems most likely, but I'm sure you have other enemies, as well."

"Not ones who would hire a pair of choppers to sink my boat." His turned-down lips mourned the death of the yacht.

"Your boat sank because it was too pretty. Next time, have an ugly boat." Ugly things seemed to last forever.

"How about we avoid a next time?"

"Then stop making enemies."

He glared. Marina proffered Darren a serene smile.

Out whipped his hand, palm raised. "Stop changing the subject and give me the damn phone."

He'd finally grasped that she stalled. She also wasn't handing over the phone. "As far as the world knows, you are dead. Get used to it. No calls. No emails. Nothing."

"What about you? How come you get to be alive and call people?"

"Because I am not being targeted."

"How can you be sure? How do I know those helicopters weren't after you? You're the one, after all, with a chip in her body."

A deactivated chip. The wound in her arm? When she'd cleaned it in the washroom of the changing area, she'd plucked out the remnants of the chip. She was off-grid.

"I have no enemies."

"Says the assassin."

"I am serious. I have no enemies because I eliminate those who would harm me."

"Seems like a rather aggressive strategy."

"I am still alive, aren't I?"

Darren shook his head. "Who are you?"

"Definitely not Francesca Parron anymore." Her lips twisted. "Thanks to you, that identity is screwed."

"Boo fucking hoo."

"Your sarcasm is not appreciated. I spent a lot of time cultivating Francesca, not to mention my modeling career."

"What's it like, living a fake life?"

Lonely at times. Especially when she couldn't be herself. But that sounded like whining, and Marina didn't whine. "My life is great, and it will be even better once I finish this job and get to spend all the money I'm making."

At the reminder of the growing bill, he grimaced.

"Speaking of the job, exactly how are you going to keep me alive if someone is targeting me? I assume, since I can't use my real name, you've got a plan? And how will we get more money?"

"Sergei will acquire new identities for us to use temporarily." Never to be used for too long and, once done, the information wiped. Only the short-lived left any traces behind.

"What makes you think I want to work with Sergei?" he asked.

"You hired me."

"You. Not him."

Time to explain how it worked. "You hired my services. Those include support from a team. Sergei is the leader of that team. He gives me my orders."

"No. *I* give you the orders."

Darren was so cute when he thought he was in charge. She patted his cheek. "You will do as I say. And I will do as Sergei tells me." Because rogue agents didn't get bonuses or a nice flat in St. Petersburg. They did sometimes get an early and quite permanent retirement.

"Like fuck am I doing what some stranger orders."

"As long as you are in my care, you don't have a choice."

"Fine, then you're fired."

She couldn't help but pat this cheek again. "Nice try. That won't stop me from protecting you. You're not the only one paying for your protection."

He blinked. "What's that supposed to mean?"

"Someone told Sergei to keep you alive."

"Who?"

She shrugged. "We don't know who it was. But they are paying us well."

"Someone hired you to protect me, and you didn't think to tell me?" He seethed the words through his teeth.

"Did you think to ask?" She said it despite knowing it would make him snap. Men were fairly predictable in that respect.

"Ask? Who the hell are you? You don't make sense at all. Everything that comes out of your mouth is the complete opposite of what it used to be."

"Because that was Francesca. Now, you are dealing with me, Marina." Her lips tugged into a half smile. "Thanks to you, I no longer have to pretend." She wouldn't hide her strength or bow to his pressure and demands. He thought she worked out of duress, and while it did play a part, she mostly did her missions, and did them well, because that was her job and she enjoyed it.

"Admitting to a split personality?"

"I am a woman of many layers." And he was a man who apparently couldn't handle it.

"Well, I don't care what you think. I still want the phone," he stated suddenly. "I need to check on my people. Make sure they made it off the island alive."

"I will ask Sergei when I call. He'll know. He can find out anything you want to know. It's because of him that I know of your secret love for Prince music. Sergei even managed to get an audio of you singing 'Little Red Corvette' in the shower."

"You're not being funny," he muttered.

"If I am attempting to be humorous, you will know, and you will laugh because it will be amusing."

He glared. Which was only right given she'd not said anything entertaining.

Sulking because she wouldn't give in, Darren stared out the window. She took that reprieve to make some phone calls, keeping the dialogue in Russian for privacy. When Sergei answered with a barked, "Wrong number," she quickly spoke.

"It's me, Marina."

"Where are you? We are having trouble with your signal."

"I went for a swim in the ocean with the client."

"This is not a vacation. You are supposed to be protecting the man, not working on your tan."

"We were attacked." She quickly detailed what had happened, and Sergei exclaimed more than once. At the end, he laughed. "You brought the client to a naked beach."

"You're missing the more important point. Someone is really trying to kill him."

"Good thing he hired you, then."

"Actually, he thinks he can fire me. I made it clear he has to obey."

"I am sure he enjoyed that."

Nope. Darren still moped. "Did his bodyguard—and fake girlfriend—make it off the island?"

"Yes. There were only a few casualties from the fire, which is where they presume Darren was consumed. They also never found Stefanov."

Which wasn't a huge loss. She was pretty sure the man was in cahoots with the island ringleader, the one most everyone had labeled Mastermind.

A pretentious title. Thus far, he'd eluded detection, but Marina was on the case. She jabbed Darren with her toe and said in English, "Your people are safe. They think you are dead."

"Thanks." Begrudgingly spoken.

She switched back to Russian. "I'm going to need some supplies."

"Tell me what you want." She made a list and, at the same time, got an address for an airfield nearby. When she hung up, Darren addressed her.

"What was that about?"

"Making plans to protect you."

"Sergei again?"

"Yes. He says hi, that he's making arrangements, and to expect a very large bill."

"I'm already paying you five thousand bucks a day."

"Plus expenses."

"What expenses?"

"Anything we require in the course of our mission."

"But I fired you."

"You don't want to fire me."

"Don't be so sure about that."

She flashed him a grin. "You won't fire the woman who is going to keep you alive."

"Who just recently wanted me dead?"

She shrugged. "I freely admit that I can be bought. Pay me enough, and I'll switch sides."

"That's very mercenary."

"It's called playing the free market."

"Surely you must have some lines you won't cross."

Marina paused to think about it a moment. "One line. I don't kill children. Unless they bite. Petrov used to bite until I broke all his teeth."

He blinked at her. Most likely in awe. She knew Petrov certainly never bothered her again, nor did any of the other children.

"What size are you?"

"What does it matter?" he asked. "It's not like we can go shopping."

"Not in person, but there are places online." She fiddled around with the browser on the phone and ran a few orders through the online shopping cart. She finished just as they slowed down. The taxi approached a small airfield.

She tossed a few bills from the wallet she'd confiscated before getting out. The driver would remember them, but by the time anyone asked, hopefully, it wouldn't matter.

Darren stood by her side as the taxi drove away. "Now what? Can we hire a pilot, do you think?"

"No need. We already have a plane reserved." Sergei was just that good. She strode toward the office.

He kept pace. "Where are we flying to?"

"You'll see."

She quickly did the little paperwork needed, and in moments, they were headed toward a two-prop plane. A little hopper that had him slowing his step. "It only seats two people."

"Very observant."

It took him only a half-second longer to figure out why the plane only had two seats.

"Dear God, you're the pilot!"

She smiled. "I am. I got my license last month."

CHAPTER EIGHT

THERE ARE MANY THINGS THAT COULD MAKE A MAN nervous in his life. Waiting for test results—especially when they involved your man junk. Wondering if the broken condom would have repercussions. And finding out you were about to put your life, much too high above the solid ground, in the hands of the slightly crazy Russian broad you once used to sleep with who thought flying when the enemy had helicopters was a good plan!

"You cannot seriously think this is a good idea."

Fran waved a hand at him and had one argument for his rant. "Don't be a baby."

"I am not being a baby!" he yelled, being a baby. At the realization, he clamped his lips, took a few deep breaths through his nose then, more calmly, said, "This plan of yours is fucking insane."

"You know what your problem is," she said, checking the plane, running her hand over the body, looking beneath it at the wheels and undercarriage. "You don't like other people in charge. You have control issues."

"I know. It's why I'm the fucking boss."

"At your school, yes. Perhaps even at Bad Boy because of your friend Harry. But not with me. You cannot tell me what to do." She stood and faced him, and while she bore the face of the woman he'd once loved, she was a harder version, assertive on a level he'd not often met even among men. She didn't back down. She stuck to her guns, and damned if he didn't respect that.

It was also a lot hotter than it should have been.

He crossed his arms. "Enjoying being the boss has nothing to do with the fact that I'd like an experienced pilot if I'm going to risk my life."

"You are just chicken to have a woman fly you."

"It has nothing to do with your gender."

"Are you sure? Because I have to wonder if you see me piloting as emasculating. Kind of like riding bitch on a bike." She jabbed his male ego.

He knew she did it on purpose. Knew she goaded him. He still walked into the trap. "I am not sexist."

"Then prove it. Get in the plane."

She didn't leave him a choice.

He sighed and clambered in. Cinched the seatbelt tightly around his waist. The helmet he had to put on didn't reassure. *Real planes don't use helmets.* The goggles were kind of cool, though. If he had a phone, he would have taken a selfie and sent it to Marcus for shits and giggles.

Through the headset, he could hear Marina chattering to herself in Russian. Going through a preflight checklist most likely. He peeked around and tried to not imagine the metal frame as a coffin.

"How far is it?" he asked, interrupting her.

"A full tank of gas."

"Which takes us how far?"

"Depends on the winds."

"Would it kill you to tell me what bloody airport we're going to?"

"Possibly, which means it's best not to take a chance."

If the plane weren't already moving, he might have reached forward to throttle her. As it was, his fingers clutched instead at the seat as the plane taxied, picking up speed, jostling and bouncing as it moved.

When the weightless sensation hit, he stared straight ahead. Reminded himself that thousands of airplanes flew safely each day. Although, when they crashed...

A reminder that didn't help with his nerves. What goes up, always comes down. Hopefully, not hitting the ground and exploding into flames.

Rather quickly, the plane evened out. Marina chuckled. "You can breathe now."

After he'd taken a breath, he said through gritted teeth, "I'm fine."

"Just remember, this is safer than a helicopter."

"The last helicopter ride I went on, the pilot jumped out, and I almost died."

She snorted. "Only because your last bodyguard wasn't as well trained as I am."

"Marcus is an ex-soldier, not an assassin. And I'll have you know, he landed our asses just fine."

"I would have done it better."

"You can pilot a helicopter?" he asked, the query heavy with skepticism.

"I can drive anything."

"Including me mental," he muttered, turning his head to peek out the window.

The midafternoon sun beat down on the world below them, the land vibrant and lush, parceled into sections bisected by the roads. The vehicles among them like ants creeping. The bright blue spots of pools and orange roofs provided contrast to all the greenery. And around all the land...water. Ocean to the left and the right, the narrow island keys surrounded by the sea. It reassured him a little to see that they weren't going back out over open water. Brazen aerial attacks seemed less likely when flying above land. More eyes, more radar. They had some measure of safety.

I shouldn't even be worrying about this kind of shit. What the hell is going on? Who is targeting me and the other academy owners?

Had some crazy individual decided to declare war on mercenaries? Seemed kind of stupid, especially since they were hiring mercenaries to complete the job.

Something was missing. Some vital clue that might make sense of it all. He tried running various scenarios through his head, but none made sense.

You know what else didn't make sense? Fran's words spoken suddenly in his earpiece.

"Can you repeat that?" he asked. "Because I could have sworn you said to reach under the seat, grab the backpack, and put it on."

"Or don't. But landing intact will be harder without a parachute." Spoken as she wiggled around in the seat in front of him, putting on some gear.

"Why would I need a parachute?" he barked as he leaned over and groped under his seat. His fingers latched on to a canvas bag. "I thought you knew how to fly?" The plane showed no signs of distress as it coasted along.

"I know how to fly."

"Is this where you tell me you failed landing?" he muttered as he tried to stab his arms through the straps. The seatbelt impeded him, and he had to unbuckle to lean forward enough to get the pack on.

"I passed landing. I did, however, fail fuel consumption. Never was good at math."

Stutter. The engine faltered.

His blood ran cold.

"Did you fuck up the gas?"

"No. I knew we'd run out." She peered over her seat at him. "Which is why we need to get out now."

"But I don't want to jump." Someone take his damned man card. He was okay with it if he could land in this plane, in one piece.

"Don't be chicken. We'll be perfectly safe. The parachutes are almost entirely foolproof."

"Almost?"

"Sometimes, one fails." He could hear the nonchalant shrug in her words. "It's life."

"Can't you just be Fran for one single second? Just one," he shouted.

The engine died, and all he heard was the whistle of the wind as she looked at him. Her features softened. Her lip trembled. "I'm scared, Darren. I don't know what to do. Save us."

The sudden switch from in charge to completely submissive hit him hard. No wonder this new Fran mocked him. The Fran he knew in France was a complete sock puppet to his ego, pandering to his alpha personality, catering to his every need.

A complete sham, and he realized that as nice as Fran was, Marina—with her brusque manners and confidence—was even better.

Imagine having this dominant lady in bed.

It was totally the wrong time for a hard-on and epiphanies. "If I live, I'm going to kill you," he grumbled as he opened the door and gulped at the air rushing below him.

"And here I was going to say we should have sex to celebrate our safe landing." With those shocking words, she flung herself out of the plane, an aircraft sputtering as the engines died.

He paused, staring out the door. The engine gave one last cough, and then there was only the sound of the whistling wind. How long could the breezes keep the plane aloft?

"Chicken!" He heard her faint mocking. With a big sigh, he dove out of the plane, too.

He closed his eyes against the rushing wind. His goggles protected him, but he didn't want to see the horizon rushing at him. If he fucked up, that ground wasn't going to be his friend.

Please don't let them have to scrape me off the ground and use dental records to identify me.

He knew enough from seeing videos and movies to put himself in a starfish, making himself larger to slow his descent. The rushing air buffeted him, and he heard Marina laughing. Fucking laughing. That was the only reason he opened his eyes.

She coasted under him, her stolen summer dress rippling around her body, her hair streaming from its ponytail with the wind.

She yelled, the words carried away by the breeze and almost unintelligible. "Pull your cord in five. Four."

Fran got to one, and he saw her body twitch. Gyrate. She rolled, and he saw her yanking to no effect.

Meanwhile, he still held his cord. He let it go and called himself all kinds of stupid as he narrowed his body into an arrow. He gathered speed, aiming for her, knowing the ground rushed more quickly. Saw her watching him come for her without panic in her gaze. How could she not be scared? His heart raced a mile a minute, his mind screamed at him to save himself.

Darren held out his arms and tried to slow his descent as impact with her body neared. They still collided hard, knocking the breath from him as her body wrapped around him spider style, arms and legs cinching him. Then there was a jolt. She'd found and yanked the cord for his chute, and the fabric snapped out over them, catching the air currents, slowing their rushing descent, and preventing a dual splatter.

He heaved out a shaking breath.

Marina—not Fran, not this bold woman—laughed, her breath warm against the skin of his neck and ear. "Nice catch."

"I'm going to kill you when we hit the ground."

"Kill me with your mighty cock?" The dirty words tickled his lobe.

Shocked him, and aroused. "What the hell, Fran?"

"It's Marina. And I like it rough."

With those words, she sprang away from him in a flip, and a moment later, her chute emerged, a billowy white cloud springing from her back.

She'd played him.

Again.

He kept underestimating her. No more. It was time he caught up and entered the game. Time to show her who was boss.

CHAPTER NINE

THERE WAS SOMETHING LIBERATING AND TERRIFYING about free falling. The realization that you could smash into the ground and not walk away was the thing every skydiver thought about. Especially those afraid of heights.

Marina hated heights. Always had, which meant she fought harder than most to overcome it. The fact that flying made her nervous was why she'd learned to pilot. She made herself learn to parachute and even hang-glide because she refused to let fear control her.

Yet wasn't it cowardice that had her fleeing Darren in Paris?

The man couldn't hurt her, not physically, but she was smart enough to recognize there was something about him, about the way he felt for her, that could ruin her. *He could be the chink in my armor against the world.* The worm wiggling its way into her heart and changing her life's course.

Thoughts of Darren kept her mind occupied as the winds tugged at her chute, slowing her descent. The land rushed fast to meet her, eager to say hello.

While expecting the jolt, it still caused her to grunt as her feet hit the ground hard, and she did a bit of a run forward to keep the chute from smothering her.

Darren had obviously never jumped before. She heard him cursing and looked back to see him covered in fabric, cussing and shoving and then glaring when she finally freed him.

"I don't like you," he muttered. "That was a shitty thing to do."

"But necessary. And admit it, wasn't it just the teensiest bit fun?"

"Worrying that I'm about to die is not fun."

"Then you should try to avoid that. If it's your time, then nothing you do will stop it. So...you might as well enjoy life."

"How about I enjoy life on solid ground?"

"Where would the fun be in that? Grab your chute and bring it over here. We need to hide it from view." The field they'd landed in didn't have much cover; however, it did have a ditch overgrown with weeds and bushes that they could shove their gear in where a casual glance wouldn't spot it.

Then they had to walk. Given that they'd dived out of the plane a few minutes later than expected—because Darren had balked at her orders—they didn't land in the field she'd planned, forcing them to hike two miles to where the car Sergei ordered was waiting.

He grumbled the whole way. "I can't believe you

fucked with me like that. I thought you were going to die."

It shouldn't have warmed her jaded heart that he cared, but it did. Even worse, his disgruntlement over the prank she'd played—the old parachute-doesn't-work joke—was cute. He acted as if she'd done something horrible. And maybe she had.

When she did it, a part of her had wondered what he would do. He hated her, or so he kept claiming. But despite his feelings, he'd tried to save her. Which said what about him? That he harbored a hero complex, or that he still gave a damn about her despite everything she'd done?

Does he still care? He'd better not, because she certainly didn't. She pretended not to hear the lie.

She didn't look at him as she said, "I'm surprised you saved me. I would have thought letting me die would have soothed your ego."

"I should have let you splatter. I hear meat chunks make for good fertilizer."

"That's not very nice."

"Neither is forcing me to jump from a plane."

"Don't be such a pussy. Live a little."

"How about instead of living a little, we try living a long life?"

"I'd die of boredom," she muttered as they finally reached the car, exactly where Sergei had said it would be. Marina reached under the wheel well, fingers dancing along the inside of the frame until she found the magnetic box. The key fob inside made the lights on the car flash, and the trunk clicked before it eased open on a mechanical hinge.

"How the hell did you manage all this?" he said. "This took planning."

"Sergei is a good handler." He made sure Marina had what she needed before she even knew it was required. It was why she made sure to buy him the biggest, most expensive bottle of vodka she could find every holiday season. It didn't pay to be cheap with the man who often held your life in his hands.

Inside the trunk, she found clothes, cash, and identification with credit cards. There was even a box packed with food.

Darren shook his head with each item she gave him. "This is ridiculously efficient," he said, looking at his likeness on a driver's license calling him Stewart Brown.

"Doesn't your academy teach operations?"

"Yes. But this"—he shook the driver's license bearing his face—"is faster than I'm used to seeing."

"That is because your friend running Bad Boy Inc. is too nice. He should push his people harder."

"What do you know about BBI?"

"I know plenty. But the basics are that they are an agency like the one I work for, but one more caught up in following rules than we are."

"What's that supposed to mean?"

"We don't mess around when we need something."

"Neither do we, but we're also not stupid or dicks about it."

Marina shrugged. "And that is why you're not as efficient. Sometimes, you have to be a dick."

"At what expense, though? Some things can't be bought."

"In life, there is a price for everything."

"Bullshit. You can't put a price tag on morals or doing the right thing." Darren changed clothes as they talked. He poured water from a bottle onto the shirt he'd removed, using it as a rag to wash himself. Sergei had thought of everything, including water, protein bars, and toothbrushes.

Darren rubbed the wet shirt over his face, scrubbing it, the growth of an overnight beard adding a rugged dark line to his jaw. "Well?" he asked. "Do you have any? Morals, that is?"

"I have lines." She didn't elaborate. His jaw tightened. She almost smiled.

"BBI and all the academy students abide by a certain code. For one, we don't kill innocent women and children."

"Which seems rather shortsighted. I've known some pretty violent women in my time." Children, too. Those raised to think killing was okay were hard to bring back from the edge. She'd never intentionally gone out to kill a child. However, she wasn't averse to dropping them off at a place that knew how to rehabilitate boys and girls. They made the best soldiers for the state.

"A violent woman isn't what I'd call innocent."

"What if circumstances shaped her? Where do you draw the line? Who gets to decide?"

His lips flattened. "You're twisting my words."

"No, merely pointing out the inanity of them. Very few people are innocent in this world."

"Is this your way of justifying murder?"

"I don't need justification if I'm getting paid." She copied Darren's wipe-down trick, stripping to her bra then slathering the wet shirt over her skin. She caught him looking. He quickly turned, pretending disinterest.

The key point being he pretended. Much as he tried to hide it, she could tell that Darren found himself attracted. His semi-erection pointed to that fact. Literally.

She swapped into more familiar clothes: black jeans, turtleneck, and boots. "You can stop hiding. I'm decent now."

He turned and eyed her. "I hope that's not supposed to be inconspicuous. You look like a cat burglar."

"That is a very sexist thing to say, considering this is proper bodyguard wear. All black." She skimmed her hand down her body, drawing attention to the holster that hugged her rib cage, making her left breast appear more prominent.

"A guy with a bodyguard is going to stick out, especially a guy with a girl protecting him."

"That wasn't an issue when you brought Kacy with you to the island." When she'd first seen Darren with the petite Latina, she'd felt a hot surge of anger. A how-dare-he moment that went away once she noticed that Kacy was there to guard—not sleep with—Darren. She didn't care to examine why she experienced jealousy.

"No one knew Kacy was my bodyguard because she pretended to be my girlfriend."

"Is that your subtle way of asking me to climb into your bed?"

"Would you?"

She eyed him, and he boldly stood there, arms crossed over his chest, his jaw squared.

"Keep looking at me like that, and I will climb you right now." She winked, and he might have growled. Very sexy.

"This is not the time to play games."

"Because you know I'll win."

"Were you always this argumentative?"

"You mean assertive. And, no, I wasn't in Paris. For you, I was a simple girl, basking in your attention." She batted her lashes. "Very annoying."

"Depends on which side of it you were on," he muttered. "We're getting off track. We were talking about your very public display of protection. I thought you wanted the fact that I'm still alive kept a secret. This..."—he gestured to Marina and then himself —"people will notice."

"Probably, but it will take time to filter through channels."

"You talk like you want the person after me to find us."

For a smart man, he seemed to miss the whole logic of it. "Of course they have to find us. How else will we stop them? But this way, I can control the how and when of it."

"By using me as bait." He paused in the midst of putting on his new shoes to scowl at her.

"Yes. A big, strong man like you surely doesn't mind."

"Don't you pull that shit with me."

"Are you going to say no?" She smiled, the taunt in it clear.

"You know I won't." A grumble in his reply. "But I think we should call in my team to help."

"What if they're compromised?"

"What if your people are?"

"Then we'd already be dead."

"We almost did die." He glanced at the sky.

She snorted. "People skydive every day."

"I don't."

"Your loss."

"You crashed the fucking plane."

"I had to. If someone does figure out that we made it to shore alive, they'll be looking for us. They might trace us to that airport. The fiery remains will keep them guessing for a while."

"And you don't think that's a little extreme?"

She gave him a most serene, "No."

"What else do you have planned to muddy our trail? Going to torch this car when we're done?" He slapped the trunk. "Maybe bomb a hotel?"

"We could if you want to. Sergei can quote you a price."

He frowned. "I'd better not be paying for that plane. That was your idea to crash it."

"To protect you. You're welcome."

"There were other ways we could have handled that."

"My way is best."

"I am going to kill you." A threat he kept repeating and yet hadn't acted on.

"If that is a euphemism for sex, then we should probably wait until we reach the hotel. There are mosquitoes out here. I wouldn't want your delicate skin harmed."

The dark look Darren shot her way had Marina replying with a wink.

"I am going to kill you twice." A quietly voiced threat without heat said a moment before he slammed shut the passenger door of the car.

At least he didn't try and take the wheel. Most men had a thing about women driving them because, apparently, they saw the road better. Utterly false. A survey by some insurance group said that men were much more likely to die in a car crash than women.

"Where are we off to?" he asked as she put the car in drive and got them away from the deserted area.

"Somewhere."

"Could you elaborate?"

"Probably."

He waited before growling, "Would you stop doing that?"

"Doing what?"

"Being deliberately fucking obtuse. Tell me where we're going."

"To a hotel."

A sigh left him. She expected him to freak out, yell at her, and demand answers, but he surprised her. "What are you trained in? Any more hidden skills I should know about?"

"You should ask, Sergei. He has a list."

"Give me the basics."

She began to tick them off. "Hand-to-hand combat in numerous styles, knife throwing, heavy artillery, including tanks—"

Darren interrupted. "As in a great big, metal tank?"

"Is there any other kind?"

"Why the hell would you need to know how to drive a tank?"

She shrugged. "I don't know, but if it is required, then I can handle it." It was also extremely fun. "I can pilot a helicopter, parachute, hang-glide—"

"Knit. Cook. Surf." He rolled his eyes.

She held up a hand. "No surfing." Stupid sport was only about balance. She had great balance on the beam, but put her on a floating plank, and she fell over every time!

"Do you like working for your agency?"

"Is this another ploy to try and get me to defect to Bad Boy Inc. or some other agency?"

"No. I doubt you'd be a good fit."

A truth that, for some reason, stung. "Good, because I'm not interested. Why all the questions about my skills?"

"I'm just curious. You obviously had a different education than what we offer via the academy."

"I am slightly more educated than most. I was an apt learner."

"And do you enjoy the job?" he asked. "The majority of our graduates seem to like their field of work. We have a pretty good retention rate, considering what we do."

"There is much I like about it. Some things, not as

much. Keep in mind that my feelings on the matter weren't ever really considered. I had no choice. This is what I was trained for. People put in time and money to give me these skills, which means there is a debt to be repaid, a debt that needs more than Russian minimum wage."

"They set a price for your training?"

"Someone has to pay for it."

"Surely by now, with all your missions, you've paid it off."

"It is a very large obligation." The kind that had interest compounding it. "Don't your students pay to learn?"

"My students owe the academy nothing. Most are handpicked from the streets. We look for potential, not people with deep pockets."

"If they don't pay, then how does your academy stay in business?"

"Private donations by certain investors who want to ensure that there are quality people out there they can hire. The agencies like Bad Boy and others also pay per diem when they take graduates."

"So, your students don't have to pay anything at all?" She scoffed. "No wonder they don't work as hard."

"They work plenty hard."

"I work harder."

The noise he made wasn't quite an I'll-kill-you sound, but it was close. She reached over and turned on the radio, cranking it. She needed to pay attention to the road and not argue with him—because it was too fun, and distracting.

Darkness fell quickly this time of year, early spring. Her headlights provided the only illumination on the country road. The car had a built-in navigation system, but she didn't need the GPS to guide her. She knew the place they were going because she'd used it before. Just shy of ten o'clock, after doing a series of turns that kept them off the main roads—where cameras might be watching—she pulled in front of a many-storied luxury hotel. She stopped under the portico, the kind with a valet.

The servant in uniform attended Darren—who fit the part of rich owner with his casual shirt and slacks, both expensive. Marina took her time exiting the car, eyes scanning the darkness past the bubble of light. She did it mostly out of habit, as she doubted anyone would have picked up their trail already.

Popping the trunk, she leaned against it as the bellboy took charge of their meager luggage. A case for each of them. Darren's much larger, of course, being the client. She slipped the bellboy a some cash then followed Darren inside. He went straight to the registration desk.

The attendant, a fine-boned male, proffered a bright smile. "Hello, sir, and welcome."

"Evening. I need a room, please." Darren had a modulated voice and perfect manners.

"We have plenty available," said the man behind the desk.

"Sergei called ahead," she muttered to Darren. She peeked around his shoulder to say, "We have a reservation, under Brown."

The young man's fingers clacked as he typed on his keyboard. "Here is it. A suite on the eighth floor. Queen bed and—"

"Nope, that won't do." Darren shook his head. "I want the penthouse."

"Let me see if it's available, sir."

As the man scurried off, Marina scanned the lobby. "The penthouse? I didn't take you for a spoiled rich boy."

"Better amenities."

"This isn't a luxury vacation."

"I'm paying for it."

True.

In short order, they were upgraded, and the bellboy, with their luggage, escorted them to the top floor. The penthouse level was keycard access only. Ridiculously easy to bypass, but it made the rich folk happy.

The suite was fairly open and fully equipped, including a stark white kitchen, the marble tops gleaming brightly. It overlooked the dining room with its shining, teak wood, six-person set. The massive, curved couch faced the panoramic windows with a view of the ocean. The wrap-around balcony didn't impede the panorama at all with its glass railing. Given the time of night, all they saw were the lights of boats dotting the water. By day, they'd get an expansive sea view.

Tipping the bellboy again, Marina ushered him out, securely locked the door to ensure no surprises, added a chair under it for good measure, then kicked off her boots before hitting the kitchen. "What are the chances it's stocked?" she asked.

"It'd better be at this price," Darren said before he wandered toward the wall of windows, prompting her to say, "Let's not make you a target for snipers."

"You're about as much fun as Kacy was. I'm going to have a shower." He began stripping before he'd even hit the bedroom, shrugging off his shirt before slamming the door shut.

She sighed into the fridge. "And the cupboard is bare."

They'd have to order food. First, though, she took a quick shower in the other bathroom. Marina was munching on a protein bar from her suitcase when Darren finally emerged wearing shorts hanging low on his hips. His skin gleamed, still damp from the water, and his hair stood in wet spikes. She'd opted to scrape hers back into a tight bun. She had also changed into athletic shorts and a tank top for ease of movement.

He flung himself into the chair across from her and grimaced. "Does this place have any Advil? That was way too much swimming today."

"Old," she coughed before eating another bite of her almond and honey oat bar.

"I'm not even forty."

"And you won't reach fifty if you don't take better care of yourself."

"Says the woman who's not even twenty-five. Must be nice to be in a position to judge."

"Thirty-four, actually," she said before sipping from the water she'd found in the mini bar.

"But you told me..." He glared. "Was anything you said the truth?"

"My teachers said a mixture of truth and lie is the best as you are less likely to mess up the details."

"How much of what you told me as Fran was true? Your dog, Tipoux?"

"Fake. Animals are expensive and needy, plus the agency doesn't allow them."

"Your love of croissants?"

"That was real. They are evil. And delicious." It was why she'd given him morning blowjobs with the promise that he'd bring her back some.

"You are nothing like the Fran I met in Paris."

"Because that woman wasn't the real me." She shrugged. "I gave you what you wanted."

"And what is it you think I want?"

"A woman who is sweet and soft-spoken. Who hangs on your every word. Who laughs at your jokes." She uttered a false giggle. "Who doesn't remind you of the killers your academy trains."

"I am not ashamed of what the school does."

Her head tilted. "Yet you are most judgmental about my choices."

"Because of pride. You fooled me. I am trying to get past that."

His honesty startled. "Why do you want to get past that?"

He shrugged. "Maybe because you're right. It isn't cool for me to act like a dick about your job. But I think I'm allowed some leeway, given your occupation revolved around me."

"You are a popular man." Still very sexy, too.

She hadn't lied before about bedding him because of

his looks. Then she kept coming back for more because it was just that good. Her body remembered. It shivered and begged her to dive onto Darren. To mash her mouth to his in the hopes he would make her body sing like he used to.

Doubtful he'd agree. They'd barely moved past the hate. Any attempt on her part would be rebuffed. But it didn't hurt to try.

"Now that we're here in relative safety, what's the plan? You said you wanted to use me as bait. How is that going to work?"

"No idea. Sergei hasn't told me yet."

He blinked at her. He had really nice lashes for a man. Thick. Dark. His eyes, smoldering. His lips... She stared at them and realized they moved.

"...let someone else make that kind of decision."

She held up her hand. "Stop. No more talking."

"You can't just—"

"Shhh." She waved the hand. "Just sit there and look pretty. I will take care of it." Once Sergei advised her. Mavericks didn't last long in this field, despite what the movies said. A good handler kept his field agent alive.

Darren sputtered. "Look fucking pretty? What the hell is that supposed to mean?"

"Such dirty language." She dropped the hand. "Did you mean to say, let's fuck?"

He clamped his lips. "I am never sleeping with you again, Fran."

"Good, because Fran is gone. Now it's me who wants to give you a try." She winked. She expected him to flee.

He remained in his seat. Angry. Stiff. Leaning

forward and growling, "Since you obviously want to, let's do it."

It took her a moment to grasp that he'd agreed. That wasn't supposed to happen. She was supposed to goad him into getting angry enough to stalk off. Thereby, making it easy for her to resist him.

"You don't mean that."

"I do." He shoved back from the table and gestured to his groin. "Let's go at it. Right here. Right now."

"I have to do my rounds."

"Do them after."

"You need sleep."

"I sleep better after sex." He stood and held out his hand. "If you're in bed with me, I'll be safe. No one can get to me."

True. And sex with him was bound to be good; however, she didn't trust him. Wondered at his motive. He seemed too calm about it.

Do it. Her body had no qualms.

She got to her feet. "What happened to no sex?"

"Can't a man change his mind?" He reached out and grabbed her, dragged her close enough to tug her into his lap.

A lap she'd missed.

His large hand cupped the back of her head, drew her close. Really damned close. She flattened her hands on his chest, felt the steady thump of his heart. He remained shirtless, meaning her fingers pressed against firm flesh. The heat of him scorched. He drew close enough that his breath feathered her lips.

She swallowed. Anticipation made her tingle. Her

sex pulsed with need. She moved first, slanting her lips over his. Sighing in remembered pleasure.

I missed this. Missed him.

Which made his next actions all the more frustrating. He stood, dumping her from his lap, ending the kiss with a gruffly spoken, "You know what, I changed my mind again. I don't want sex with you."

He turned away, and she couldn't help but exclaim, "Get back here and finish what you started."

"No can do. See, unlike you, I have a few lines, and one of them is that I don't fuck my staff." His bedroom door slammed.

Her pussy cried.

But a part of her also admired him and said, "Bravo." Admired this harder version of Darren.

I like a challenge. Game on.

CHAPTER TEN

DARREN'S DICK ACHED. IT ALSO CALLED HIM STUPID.

Why did I walk away?

She wanted him. He wanted her. So what the fuck was he doing in this room while she remained out there?

I'm being smart and not falling twice for her scam. She'd well and truly fooled him the first time with fake Fran. No way would he get sucked in by Marina. He'd meant what he said. He didn't fuck his staff.

Technically, I fired her.

However, she'd refused to quit the job, and he admittedly needed some help. He'd gotten rid of Marcus, who truly wasn't equipped to protect him from the higher-level mercenary stuff. He wouldn't put his friend in any more danger. Just like he couldn't keep Kacy working for him even if she was a pro. She and Marcus had only just discovered their feelings for each other. Darren wouldn't get in the way of that, and neither would he call to hire someone else because...

Admit it. Having Fran/Marina as my bodyguard is much more fun than someone recommended by BBI.

Being around her made him feel alive in ways that proved addictive. She kept throwing him for loops. Set his pulse racing. That said, he needed to get a modicum of control back. She seemed to think she called the shots, or that Sergei did. Darren wasn't without his own resources. He knew a person or two he could contact who wouldn't let it slip that he was alive. Someone who would know to look for him if he disappeared for real.

He used the phone on the nightstand by the bed, dialing a number that couldn't be traced and that immediately wiped all record of it happening as it went through.

"Hello, you've reached BBI. What can I help you with?" Harry's professional tone relaxed Darren. His old friend would know what to do.

"Harry, it's Darren."

To his credit, the man didn't freak. "You're supposed to be dead."

"You should know better than to believe that without a body."

"Well, if it's really you, then you know the drill."

The drill being that Darren had to use a phrase that only they knew because, sometimes, old-school tricks were the best.

He went with, "How is that kumquat plant of yours growing?"

"Well, I'll be damned. You are alive. Where are you? What happened?"

Darren spent the next few minutes giving Harry a rundown, pulling the phone as far as it could go, which was the doorway of the bathroom where he had the water running. He wasn't sure if Marina listened, and he didn't want to chance her ripping the phone from the wall.

"You need me to extract you?" Harry asked when Darren finished his story with his current location.

"No. I want to see what happens next." See what Marina had planned. "But I do want something in place just in case. Something she knows nothing about. Plane tickets, train tickets, IDs. In other words, a few escape routes."

"No problem."

"How are the wedding plans coming along?" And by wedding, he meant for Reaper and his surprising choice. A civilian, but one who had a lone wolf sister who'd shot up her fiancé. It was a complicated story and, from what he'd heard, an almost deadly match. Reaper had been told by his soon-to-be sister-in-law that if he hurt Annique, he'd die. No one doubted that Jasmine, a killer for hire, would do it.

"We've got three locations booked. Catering and flowers, too. The location will be sent out to guests the day before to ensure minimal chance of disruption."

"Excellent." That would cause confusion, especially since they planned to leak the three locations to different people in order to flush out any spies in their midst.

If they failed to catch the culprit and his trouble-causing cohorts ahead of time and trouble hit the wedding, then he could placate himself with the thought that dozens of operatives from the academy, BBI, and other mercenary agencies where Reaper was a familiar face would be in attendance.

Having that many people in one place could prove risky, yet they had to do something to flush out whoever kept fucking with them.

His phone call with Harry done, Darren threw himself on the bed. The first quiet moment he'd had since shit hit the fan on the island what seemed like a lifetime ago.

Thinking of a long time ago meant his mind veered back a few months to when he'd first met Fran.

She jostles me, a soft bump that sends my arm up, and the wine in my glass sloshes over the rim. Looking down, I cringe as I see the red stain spreading over the white silk of her dress.

I babble an apology, but she doesn't seem to care. She is laughing. Her giggle full of mirth, her lips curved into a sweet smile. Before I know it, I've got her number and she's agreed to meet me for dinner. I can hardly wait.

Dinner is amazing. Eyes bright with interest, she leans over the table, listening to me. Laughing at all my jokes. Dropping her gaze shyly. I can't help but want her.

We sleep together, and it's cock blowing. She's wilder than expected in bed. The shy girl quite wanton between the sheets. I am addicted. I neglect my work to see her. It's pathetic. Marcus remarks on it. "She's leading you around by your cock."

What if she is? Marcus doesn't understand what it's like to be in love.

Is it love? I think it is. Which is why I visit the jeweler. We're in Paris, after all, the city of love. And yes, it's quick. We haven't known each other that long. But it's long enough for me to be sure. There is a connection between us.

It's with a happy bounce in my step that I go to her building. I have a dozen perfect roses in one hand. A bag of croissants from her favorite bakery in the other. I already have a bottle of wine in her fridge.

Entering the apartment, I immediately sense that she's not home. Probably still at work. Her modeling job keeps her busy. A few times, she's even been gone overnight.

I place the flowers and pastries on the kitchen table and wander into the bedroom, only to stop dead.

The bed is perfectly made. Fran never makes it, claiming it's a waste of time since we'll just mess it up again that night. She hates chores, which is why she never picks up her clothes from the floor and hires a maid. But the maid usually comes on Mondays. The hardwood is bare, and it's only Thursday.

I don't panic yet, but I am starting to when I see that the bathroom counter, usually covered in beauty products, is also empty. My toothbrush sitting by itself on the edge of the sink.

Everywhere I look, everything is put away. No sign of clutter. No indication of anything at all. When I open the closets and cupboards, her clothes are gone, my few hanging garments lonely in the closet.

And still, I don't believe.

I can't believe.

She left me? Impossible. She wouldn't do that to me.

I am convinced that something awful has happened. Marcus thinks otherwise, but I make him look anyway. I put resources toward finding Fran before I finally admit the truth.

She's gone, and she never loved me.
Not like I loved her.

But the woman he loved never existed. Darren had loved a mirage. Marina was the true woman behind the face. He hated the reality, hated her, which begged the question: why was he working with her? Did he really think he could make her regret what she'd done?

She'd admitted that he was nothing more than a mission. A job she had sex with because she claimed she wanted to. And he almost believed it. He'd not imagined her arousal in the living room. Nor did he imagine the passion in her kiss. Surely, she wasn't *still* faking?

He wanted to rap his head off the wall for even wondering. She was off-limits.

Because I can't handle her.

What? No. He could handle her fine. He just wasn't about to reward her with good sex.

But isn't that punishing myself?

Not really. He could have any woman he liked. If that were true, then why hadn't he slept with anyone since Fran?

Because they weren't Fran. Marina wasn't Fran either. But he wanted to—

Argh. He couldn't help but growl his frustration out loud.

The door was kicked open, and in stalked the object of his strife, gun drawn.

He blinked at her. "What the fuck?"

"I heard you yell."

"And? Did I sound like I was in pain?"

"Yes." She tucked the gun into her waistband and

gave one last look around before focusing on him. "Seeing as how you're not being attacked, I am going to assume the noise was because you were jerking off and I interrupted."

"No." But only because he'd not gotten to that point yet. It usually happened in the shower when he couldn't clear his mind of Fran.

"If you're not jacking off, then why were you yelling? Were you regretting your decision to turn me down? I can see why you'd be disappointed. I am that good."

She said it with such smugness, such certainty. The worst thing? She was right. Darren had never had better. Hadn't wanted anyone since. But he wasn't about to tell her and give her the satisfaction.

"Was the sex good?" he said, feigning a loss of memory. "I don't recall."

"I see your ploy." Marina wagged a finger at him. "You regret turning me down, hence your attempt to goad me into showing you. Unfortunately for you, I took care of myself already."

"You what?"

"I had a quick second shower when you left to mope. Lucky for me, the head is detachable," she replied with a wink.

It shouldn't have made him so fucking hard. He turned away from her and paced toward the window. "Since you're here, maybe we should discuss our next move."

"Sergei—"

"Isn't here. You and I are."

"He will have a plan for us."

"What if he doesn't? Or something happens? We should have contingencies in place."

"You mean you don't have one already with Bad Boy?"

"How could BBI plan for this?" He extended his hand to the room.

"You were on the phone long enough to get things organized."

It didn't surprise him that she knew. "You spied on me."

"I didn't. That is technical work." She sounded affronted. "But Sergei let me know about it. That was very dumb."

"The number I used can't be traced."

"You do realize that you just said the impossible."

"What?" It took him a moment before he understood. If she knew about the call, then apparently, his attempts at subterfuge failed. He exclaimed, "Fuck me, how did Sergei manage to do that?" There was nothing worse than realizing he'd been out-teched.

"We are just that good. Which means, you should forget any plans you're concocting. Mine will be better."

"Why not spill your strategy, and I'll be the judge of that?"

"Maybe later."

"How about now?" He might have said more, but the damned woman left the bedroom. Much as it galled, he followed. "If we're going to work together, you can't keep ignoring me."

"Then maybe you should have thought of that before acting like a selfish ass." She arched a brow.

"Is this because I wouldn't fuck you?" The pettiness of it was, well, petty.

"You scratch me, I scratch you. It's a simple concept."

"I can't believe I'm going to say this, but I'm not whoring myself out to make you happy."

"If you change your mind, let me know."

He was almost ready to change his mind now. Perhaps choke that lying, delectable mouth with his cock to stop her from saying things that drove him nuts.

A knock at the door had him frowning. "Did you order room service?"

"Too late for food from the kitchen. But I found a place that would deliver." She eased out her gun and tiptoed to the door. She peeked through the hole and waved a hand at him. "It's the pizza guy. Hand me some money."

He grabbed his wallet and pulled some bills free as she opened the door, the gun already tucked in the back of her pants.

The pizza guy, who was older and more square-jawed than a delivery boy should be, entered. The big foil bag keeping the pie warm hung at an angle. The shirt seemed too small on his chest, the expression a little too shuttered.

It made Darren's spine straighten. Paranoia?

Perhaps, given that Fran let him in with a bright, "How much do I owe you?"

The delivery guy pulled the hand not holding the pizza from his pocket, and Darren's eyes widened at the sight of the gun. A gun the guy never got a chance to raise.

Marina rammed the palm of her hand against the delivery guy's diaphragm. He gasped and reeled back. Not far, seeing as how Marina—not Fran, Fran wouldn't hurt a fly—grabbed him by the head and dropped him to the floor.

Ouch. The wrestling move quite real unlike the fakery seen on screen.

She quickly pulled a zip tie from her ass—because it certainly didn't come from a pocket—and whipped the thug's hands behind his back. Then, while sitting on the delivery guy, who was more than a pizza dude, she reached into the bag and calmly pulled out two boxes while ordering Darren around. "Shut the door."

He shut, locked, and leaned against it, staring at her. "What the fuck just happened?"

"Looks like we were already made."

"But how?" Even as he asked, he knew. *Because I made a mistake.* Darren was a man who taught others about impossible scenarios and dangerous ambushes. He didn't usually have to implement or guard against them in actuality.

"Probably when you called," she said, sliding the two boxes onto the floor. The first she opened and revealed a pepperoni pizza cut into slices. She grabbed a piece and took a big bite, her eyes shutting for a second as she let out a soft moan.

It looked delicious, and he didn't mean the pie. "What's in the other box?" he asked as he reached for a piece oozing gooey cheese.

"Open it and see."

"Is it that hard for you to tell me what you ordered?" he grumbled.

"I only ordered one pizza," she said as Darren flipped the lid on the second box, revealing...

"A bomb!"

CHAPTER ELEVEN

DARREN ACTED AS IF HE WERE SURPRISED, AND YET from the moment she'd seen the man at the door, she'd known.

"Yes, a bomb. Did they not teach the fake-out delivery trick at your academy?" she asked as she kept eating her slice of warm pizza while eyeing the wires sticking out of the flattened explosive. There was enough plastic there to make a big boom—and turn her into pink slurry.

"We don't instruct on specific gags."

"Then what do you teach? Other than how to blow your cover by calling someone I told you not to." She couldn't help but roll her eyes.

His jaw hardened. "We train agents to be innovative. Observant. We also educate them on self-preservation. That's a bomb," he said, jabbing his finger in the direction of the box with the brown package and wires. "Shouldn't we be leaving at a run to get away?"

"Why?"

"Because bombs in general aren't good for one's health, that's why."

"Don't be so melodramatic. This one is perfectly safe. He did not have time to arm it." She dug into the unconscious man's pocket and pulled out a transmitter, a tiny remote with a single button.

Darren held out his hand. "Give me that."

"Why? Afraid I'll press it." She took a big, gooey bite and intentionally smashed her thumb on the button.

A red light atop the plastic load lit up. Darren's eyes widened. She swallowed her pizza and then reached over to the box and yanked the blue wire.

The light went out.

Darren exploded. "You fucking psycho! What the hell? You could have blown us up."

"I am not suicidal."

"You pressed the button."

"Because pressing the button is fun. You should try it some time. Hold on. Let me fix it for you." She went to jab the blue wire back into the bomb, but he reached down and snatched it from her.

"Careful. That stuff can be a little unpredictable. I knew a guy who stuffed it into his pocket. It didn't end well for him." It had been considered a good thing that idiot wouldn't be able to procreate.

"I know how to handle this stuff. I am not a complete moron."

"Yet you believed I'd actually ordered a pizza to our room." She snorted. "Did it ever occur to you that the front desk should have rung us to grab the delivery? You need a keycard for this level."

"You think he killed the bellboy?" Darren glared at the body on the floor.

"Maybe, or stole the card and snuck past him. Minor details. We should be more concerned with the fact that he's here. We should have been off the radar."

"Maybe Sergei sold you out."

"Ha, it's more likely your precious BBI office has a spy."

"Harry's staff is clean."

"Doesn't mean his equipment is."

His lips pressed into a thin line. "I'm telling you right now, it's not a leak on my side."

"You keep thinking that." Then she ignored Darren to keep eating pizza and check out the guy they'd caught.

She didn't recognize him. Then again, with how big the world was, that wasn't hard to believe. He appeared in his late thirties, European descent, no identification. A frisking located a knife and two guns: the one he'd tried to use, and another in an ankle holster.

Darren paced. "We should make plans to leave."

"And go where tonight?"

"Somewhere we don't have to worry about assassins."

"He's not an assassin. Just a low-level thug."

"One with a bomb."

"Which I wager he'll tell us was given to him."

"You don't know that for sure."

"I will in a moment. He's waking up."

Marina remained perched on the man's chest. Nothing like staring at him from a position of power to set the stage.

The lids fluttered first. Followed by a groan. Then a, "what the fuck?" followed by a body buck.

Marina leaned her forearm against the man's throat. "I wouldn't move too much if I were you. Crushed necks are hard to heal from."

"Let me go or—"

"You'll what? Blow me up?" She smiled and held up the remote. "What happens if I do this?" She pressed the inactive button, and the man squealed. It was very unmanly. He obviously wasn't well trained.

"You can stop wailing like a baby. The bomb is disabled."

"You're fucking nuts," exclaimed the man.

"Why do people always say that like it's an insult?" She shook her head. "More people should be a little crazy. Then we wouldn't mind doing what has to be done." She pinched his nose and covered his mouth with her free hand.

The thug struggled, which only increased the pressure on his neck.

Meanwhile, Darren exposed another of his morality lines. "What are you doing? You're going to kill him."

"Probably, if he doesn't answer my questions." She pulled back and let the man breathe. "Who sent you?"

"Fuc—"

She whistled as she leaned on him again, waiting until his eyes were wide enough to pop from his head.

Darren paced, muttering things like, "Why me?" and "Crazy Russian."

"Calm yourself and have another slice of pizza."

He stopped pacing to glare. "Don't tell me what to do."

"Then don't tell *me* what to do. I am the expert here." She eased up on their assailant's neck and removed her hand, allowing him to breathe. "Who sent you?"

"I don't know."

She shifted her arm, and he rasped out, "I swear, I don't. All I know is I got a call to make some easy money. I was supposed to put the pizza by your door, leave, and set off the bomb."

"But you knocked."

"I thought if I got it inside, maybe I'd get a bonus."

"You thought you'd get a bonus for blowing people up." Darren dropped to his knees, angry looking. "What the hell is wrong with you?"

The man whined, "Nothing wrong with making some money."

"Man has a point," Marina said, which sent Darren shooting to his feet and pacing again.

"Why the extreme attacks? And with such incompetents." He waved a hand at the guy under her, who took offense.

"Hey, asshole—"

Thunk.

She knocked him back out and snared a fresh triangle of pizza before perching on the couch.

Darren was still talking aloud. "This doesn't make sense. Why hire a petty thug like this one?"

"They think you're weak."

He glared at her. "I might not have trained like others who did the full program, but I'm no dummy. And I'm sure as hell better than he is." He gestured to the limp body on the floor.

"We don't know that for sure. What we do know is that I am better." She stood and stretched. "You should get some sleep."

"What about the body?" He pointed.

"I will take care of it."

"Don't you mean Sergei will handle it?"

"You sound jealous."

"Ha. You wish. I am wondering, though. What does Sergei think of you sleeping with your target?"

"Sergei doesn't care who I sleep with. He reserves his jealousy for his wife. He's married with seven children."

"I wasn't jealous."

She eyed him from her spot on the couch. "It's okay if you were. I am pretty special."

"You're conceited."

"Confident."

"Arrogant."

"Assertive, and I can do this all night."

"You can do it alone. I'm going to bed."

He left.

Marina almost followed him because taunting him was fun. How far could she push him before he snapped —and got rough with her?

Marina really wanted him to touch her.

Sigh.

She ate another piece of pizza—the cheese cold and congealing but still delicious—as she fired off some texts to Sergei.

Have cleanup issue.

Get out.

It's the middle of the night.

Bomb.

Is disabled.

No, it's not!

She eyed the pizza box on the floor. The loose wire still hanging out of it, the clay molded into a large rectangle, big enough to...

Shit.

She dove off the couch, and snared her wallet on the way to Darren's room.

Barreling in, she startled him, and he sat bolt upright in bed. "What's wrong?"

"Get dressed. We have to go."

He didn't argue, simply put on a shirt and slid on his shoes. It was when he put his hands on his wallet that all hell broke loose.

An explosion ripped through the penthouse. Only the fact that they were in the bedroom saved them. Once she'd picked herself up off the floor, a peek back through the doorway showed flames licking the carpet and walls, blocking the way out. It also showed red slime dripping from the wallpaper. The petty thug wouldn't be pulling any more jobs. She shut the door.

"We can't exit that way," she said, pushing past him

to the balcony.

"Even if you brought a parachute, I am not jumping," he declared.

"This type of height is better with a hang-glider, and we don't have one of those, unfortunately."

An alarm went off as the smoke and heat tripped a sensor. He smiled. "The sprinklers will take care of the flames."

Except... None of them were going off. Stupid computer-operated machinery. Everything these days could be controlled—and hacked.

Rather than listen to Darren curse about it, she wedged a pillow at the bottom of the bedroom door to block the seam, hoping to forestall the infiltration of the choking smoke. Then, she went to work, stripping the sheets from the bed and knotting the fine linen, tying it together.

He noticed her actions and sighed. "We're climbing, aren't we?"

Yes, they were. At least down to the balcony below them where the patio door only needed a firm yank to open, and then they were exiting the room, following a stream of sleepy people down the hall as they made it to the emergency stairs and the fresh air outside.

Within the crowd, she let Darren and his great size lead, knowing they were vulnerable in the open yet protected at the same time because of the press of bodies.

"Now what?" he asked when they found a clear spot to watch the flames shooting from the penthouse windows.

"I don't know. I wasn't expecting that." Which kind of peeved her. The old decoy bomb hiding the real bomb trick. The elegant brilliance of it proved a stark reminder that Darren was making her not think straight.

"The good news is, we're unharmed and not naked this time."

"The beach was more fun than this, though, you have to admit."

"Fun for you, maybe."

"I need to make a call." Except she realized while she'd grabbed her wallet, she'd neglected the phone. It had probably melted in the explosion. She'd need to get a new one.

"Call who? Sergei? No need. While you didn't foresee this happening, I had a feeling."

"You did not."

"I did too. I'm not the only one who made a call."

'Sergei didn't betray me."

"If you say so." He looked at the billowing smoke.

"He's the one who told me to escape."

"And you don't find that suspicious? How did he know?"

She glared at him. His turn to grin. "Admit it. He's the leak."

"Sergei wouldn't hurt me, which you'd better believe because we're going to need to call him for extraction."

"Actually, we don't. Because, like I said, I had a feeling we might get screwed. Lucky for you, I have an alternative plan."

CHAPTER TWELVE

MARINA HADN'T THOUGHT TO SNARE THEIR cellphone before escaping the burning inferno—a close call that Darren preferred not to dwell on. Only seconds before, and he'd have been the one splattering his guts all over the place. The billowing smoke and flames licking out the windows served as a reminder that her quick thinking had saved him from turning into barbecued meat, as well.

However, while he'd thank her for saving his life, he had to wonder if her precious Sergei was the reason they'd been attacked in the first place. That worry was why he insisted on using his plan to get them out of there. The purchase of a burner phone allowed him to make a quick call to Harry set their planes, trains, and automobile plan in motion. It also netted them a taxi, which drove them in loops to lose any pursuit before taking them to the airport.

Screw the train—too slow, and it didn't go anywhere interesting.

Fuck driving, because that wouldn't let him get some much-needed rest.

Flying, despite their last debacle, was the way to go. Especially since his alternative plan—that he wouldn't let Marina tell Sergei about—involved first class, a warm blanket, and a glass of wine to help him sleep. Yes, sleep. And this despite the possibility that the plane could go down because of an intentional malfunction. For all he knew, a killer was aboard.

Let Marina handle it. He was napping. His body needed rest. It could only go so long without it, and he'd reached that point. Shutting his eyes, he found himself lulled by the muted roar of the engines. The slight vibration in his seat rocked him into dreamland.

Or should he call it nightmareland since he'd once again returned to the day she left him?

The moment he'd lost his man card and all self-respect. Once he realized she was gone, he'd essentially lost his shit. He rushed to the police to report Fran missing, but they no longer provided that type of service. They advised him to hit social media. He posted on all her accounts. To no avail. No one had seen her. What if she were in trouble?

The truth wasn't penetrating at that point. The empty drawers and missing suitcase were surely a cover-up of the crime.

Eventually, though, even he couldn't deny it. Fran had left and wasn't coming back.

The blow was the worst thing he'd ever suffered. He

didn't handle it with poise or dignity at all. He got drunk. Really plastered—enough that Marcus had to bribe a whole bunch of people to get him on board a plane home. Remove him from the place of his downfall.

Once home, Darren didn't snap out of it. He spent a week getting wasted. Anything to numb the stupid pain.

I loved her. She left me.

The morning he'd woken in a pile of vomit was a wake-up call. The moment he said, "Fuck this. And fuck you." No woman was worth that kind of depression. He'd been perfectly fine with himself and his life before he met her. Time to return to his happy bachelor state.

In the spirit of cleansing, he poured the booze down the sink, burned anything of his that reminded him of her—like his soft cotton T-shirt. A plain black shirt that he couldn't help but picture her wearing, the hem just hitting the tops of her thighs.

It ignited better than expected, as did the jacket she used to borrow because every time they went out, she wore a thin dress and a little sweater.

The dancing flames acted as a balm to his spirit. It gave him the reboot he needed to step back into his life. An existence going along great until she returned. That first moment he'd seen her on the island—as gorgeous as he remembered, and aloof—had resulted in an urge to grab her, shake her, and then hug her close. His emotions proved intense. Very powerful. He'd expected the hatred for what she'd done, but the lust took him by surprise.

How could he want the woman who'd betrayed him?

A raised voice snapped Darren awake. A man argued with the flight attendant, claiming that the woman beside him threatened to cut off his hand if he so much as looked at her again.

Darren would wager he knew whom the man sat with, because Marina certainly wasn't seated beside him. Partially on purpose, but mostly by circumstance. The airplane had been pretty full when Harry booked the seats, with only single seats available; meaning, they weren't together. He'd gotten first class—with the legroom and wide cushion—while Marina sat in coach, rows behind him. Far enough that he couldn't see her, even by accident. Couldn't talk to her. He should have been relieved. Instead, anxiety gripped him. It didn't matter how far away she sat. He knew she was there.

He stood and made his way to the washroom. The damned thing was smaller than a closet. A tall man, and wide too, Darren had to turn himself, arms at his sides, to finagle any room. He pulled out his phone and used it despite all kinds of FTC regulations. No matter what Marina thought, he didn't always play by the rules.

The message he tapped was short. *Nada.* As in nothing had happened. Not yet, at any rate. Halfway through the flight, and the most excitement was the guy who thought he could creep on Marina and not get schooled.

I should punch him.

The violent thought took him by surprise. Why the sudden urge to defend Marina's honor? The woman could take care of her herself.

Harry answered his text. *Laid.* Short for "*The plan we*

hatched is getting put in place." Marina might mock the work of BBI, but Darren knew their reputation on a global level. It was better than good.

Chillax. Which meant exactly what it said. Chill and relax. Wait for something to happen or instruction from Darren.

A knock came at the door along with a belligerent, "What's taking you so long?"

Sounded like the same man who'd complained to the flight attendant.

"Sir, you can't be up here. This washroom is for first-class guests only."

"The other one on board has a puker in it, which means, unless you want me to piss in the goddamned aisle, you're gonna let me use this."

More arguing ensured as Darren fake flushed and washed his hands, taking his time, hearing the flight attendant retreat with a muttered, "Fine, use it and then return to your seat."

"Shut your piehole," the man retorted.

What an asshole. Exiting, Darren bumped into the belligerent ass and whispered, "Touch her again, and I will make sure you die before the next sunrise."

The man started to bluster, "Hey, dick—"

Darren shifted his body to hide himself, acting as if to move around; meanwhile, his hand shot out and pinched a nerve on the man's neck. The belligerent male slumped as Darren turned and walked away.

"Miss," he said, spotting the flight attendant in the aisle. "A passenger has fainted. I think he's drunk." As she hurried past, he added, "You might want to put him in restraints and have him checked out. He said something while I was in the bathroom about killing us all."

Which, these days, was enough for the guy to get put in a jump seat, his movements restricted, snoring away as they finished their trip.

The plane landed in France without further incident. As they were parked, security boarded. The bleary-faced man was yanked from the jump seat and told he was coming for questioning, which resulted in him yelling about the fascist pigs who should roast if they thought to take away his rights. That earned the fellow some cuffs and frog marching.

A petty revenge, but Darren enjoyed it.

The passengers disembarked, stretching and yawning, jostling for position to exit the plane. First-class privilege meant he got to leave first. Darren pretended that he traveled alone, wheeling his suitcase behind him —his second one in less than twenty-four hours, given the one Sergei got him had burned in the fire. Which was probably a good thing. He'd ditched everything Sergei acquired as soon as he could just in case it was bugged. His new suitcase, and Marina's as well, were cobbled together before their hasty overseas flight.

No one spared Darren a second glance. The customs agent barely looked up as she stamped him through. His passport and reason for visiting—tourism—was accepted without question. He walked straight from the customs area to the taxi corridor. Only then did he turn to casually peek behind him, expecting at any moment to see Marina come sailing after him, ready to bitch him out for getting too far ahead.

Only he didn't see her. At all.

The worry didn't hit right away. Not until the lineup for passengers had thinned, and he was the only one left standing with men barking at him in French, asking if he needed a ride.

Should he leave? The plan they'd quickly hatched on their way to the airport was to pretend they didn't know each other. Not in the airport, on the plane, or once they landed. They were supposed to take separate vehicles. An attempt to muddy a trail that had his enemies looking for two people.

Although, he did ask her about the logic of it.

"Shouldn't my bodyguard be with me?"

"If I'm with you, then who will save you if they decide to ram the taxi you're in and do a dash with your bleeding body?"

"That is a very disturbing scenario."

"That's why I'm the expert."

She most certainly was, taking the plan he'd hatched with Harry and then changing it. The first part, taking a flight over, had been accomplished. Next step? Take a taxi to the hotel Harry had booked for him. Darren would register and go up to his room only long enough to drop his suitcase, then leave via a service entrance to meet up with Marina at the pastry shop they used to frequent, a place only they would know about. His concession to Marina, who seemed to think her office was clean and that it was BBI who had a mole. He couldn't wait to prove her wrong but needed to be around for that. Which made him realize she still hadn't exited the customs area.

Was she detained? Had the crazy woman smuggled a weapon on board and gotten caught?

Perhaps she'd ditched him. Decided he wasn't worth the bother.

Not a big deal either way. He didn't need her. Other resources existed. Even though he was in Paris, Harry could hook him up. Hell, if Darren put in a call to Marcus—his usual bodyguard—Marcus would move mountains to bail him out.

He stared back, hoping for a glimpse. Nothing.

Get in the taxi. Keep to the plan.

But what if he got in and never saw Marina again?

Things remained unresolved between them. He didn't like it. He needed closure.

He peeked back at the airport, still not seeing her.

What if she were in trouble?

She could take care of herself.

She could, but...what did that say about him that he wouldn't even try to check on her?

Morals. Argh. They made a man stupid. So fucking dumb, he grumbled quietly to himself as he headed back into the terminal.

He knew how it would look to her. As if he didn't trust her to do her job. Yet, he couldn't help it. The vain male part of him asked, *What if she needs me?* And then there was that nagging feeling in his gut, the one that said something was wrong.

The concourse was a bustling place. People moving, the chattering a steady hum. A man standing by himself staring in the midst of it would appear out of place. He needed a place to conceal himself and watch. A payphone on the wall by a potted plant provided great cover. Receiver to his ear, Darren faked a call. From his vantage point, he scanned the crowd, a constantly shifting scene as bodies moved erratically all over the place. Many things drew his eye, and a sudden thicker flow of people as a plane arrived and disgorged its passengers meant he almost missed her.

The men flanking Marina were big, the pair of them towering over her. The shiny pate of the tallest one gleamed under the lights. They each had a hold of her upper arms, which would have seemed normal if the men wore uniforms. But they didn't. They sported casual clothes—jeans for one, athletic pants for the other, and collared T-shirts under leather jackets. Definitely not the dark suits of security or the distinctive garb of law enforcement.

Who were these men?

Marina had her lips pressed into a flat line. Her gaze passed over him. Widened. He saw her give a little negative shake.

Don't get involved? Hell, no. The male gene demanded that he do something.

Darren hung up the phone and wandered in their direction, his rapid clip closing the gap. The trio walked briskly, and he wondered when Marina would make her move. This docile version of her didn't seem right. She probably lulled her captors as she plotted the best place to act.

Where would she make her move? Not in the terminal, that was for sure. It would draw too much scrutiny, especially these days when terror attacks were common and the reaction swift. She'd probably wait for some-place with less chance of law enforcement swarming and shooting.

Marina and her escorts exited the terminal and hit the area for passenger pickup. A blue Fiat pulled up to the curb, and the men angled toward it. Any second, he expected to see her yank free. He got closer.

The door to the car opened. Still, she did nothing, didn't even turn back to see if he was there. Marina slid into the back seat of the vehicle. The two men entered after her, one in the front, the other beside her.

Why didn't she dive out the other side?

Was one of the men Sergei?

Something hot burned in his chest, urging him to act. Do what, though? Run over there and pound on the car? Demand answers? Seemed a little over the top. Perhaps Marina wanted to go with them.

His gut said otherwise, but his instincts always said to exercise caution, which was why he swerved and headed to the median for a taxi. He flagged down a cab, yanking open the passenger door to toss in his suitcase before diving in after it.

He immediately pressed his face against the plastic shield separating front and back. "I need you to follow that blue Fiat." He jabbed a finger to this left.

The man, wearing a turban and a fabulous curled mustache, replied in heavily accented English, "No do crime."

"I am not doing anything illegal. Look, I came to surprise my wife. She works at the airport. But I saw her get into that car with some men. I think she's cheating on me."

The man's eyes widened. "Cheating bad."

"Exactly. So, can you follow them? I have money." Darren fanned some bills in the window.

"We follow." The driver slapped his meter on, and in moments, they were off, leaving Darren's stomach behind them.

Seriously, the guy drove faster than a bat out of hell.

Darren had worried they'd lose the other vehicle given it took off just ahead of them, but his driver—on a mission to help Darren catch his wife in flagrante delicto—was most earnest. He weaved through tight spots that caused Darren to a lose a few years off his life, ran a red light that sprouted a new gray hair, and then dropped to a spot two cars back from the vehicle holding Marina.

While his driver kept track of her, Darren pulled his cellphone out of his pocket. He logged into an online dating website and sent a message to a profile on it. Since he was out in the open, he was more cautious with his communication.

Made it to the city of lights. But having a hard time finding a place with vodka. Might need a recommendation.

Which was code for: in Paris, lost Marina, might need a new plan.

The phone beeped at him. *Delivery failed.* Stupid piece of junk. He'd managed to use it on a plane with some WiFi finagling, but in the middle of a city, he lost the signal.

He tucked it away and kept an eye on the things

around him. The familiar and, at the same time, alien nature of Paris struck him. This was a city where old and new cohabited. The press of age, bound into every original stone block, seeped, giving the city a majestic feel you didn't get in the colonies of the good ol' U S of A. They headed toward the Seine, the river meandering through the heart of Paris.

The buildings bordering the important waterway ranged from exclusive and expensive homes and apartments to more commercial endeavors. The farther they went from the city, the more he banked on the latter.

His phone buzzed in his pocket. The message finally delivered as the buildings thinned and the signal could make it. He'd need to gather a better phone as soon as possible.

They lost their buffer cars hiding them from the Fiat. His driver noticed and turned.

"What are you doing?" he asked, leaning forward. "You're going to lose them."

"This way better," was the heavily accented reply.

The driver took him on a parallel route. At one point, he turned and brought them back, and Darren cursed and ducked as he saw the taillights of the Fiat disappearing into a warehouse.

The rolling door cranked shut behind it.

"Stop the car by that hydrant," Darren ordered, digging into his pocket for money.

He paid his driver, who thanked him profusely once he saw the size of the tip. Darren slid out of the back of the car then stood a bit flummoxed on the sidewalk with his suitcase. What should he do now?

He looked completely out of place in this district. Overdressed, under-armed, and definitely not French, which gave him an idea.

The knock on the warehouse door took a moment to be answered. One of the thugs from the airport peered out suspiciously.

"*Qu'est ce que tu veux?*"

"I'm lost. I don't suppose you have a phone I could borrow." Darren smiled, doing his best to appear benign.

The man didn't buy it. He grabbed Darren by the collar and yanked him inside.

CHAPTER THIRTEEN

WILL HE EVER SHUT UP?

Pierrot, a short Frenchman with a shaved crown, a goatee—because it made him look artistic supposedly—and tiny Lennon glasses, still ranted, and had been since the moment his thugs escorted her inside. "The nerve of you. Thinking you can just up and leave without a word or even a thought to the mess you left behind."

"You had plenty of other girls to use. I got called for another job."

"You were already on a job," he railed. "Working for me. You ruined the show."

Highly doubtful given there were dozens of models at any time willing to work the runway. However, Pierrot took it as a personal slight. A melodramatic man to start with—most designers she'd met were—he thrived on things he could go ballistic about. A model gaining a few pounds before a show. The makeup artists not grasping his vision. Marina not sticking around to model one of his precious creations. That and more was enough to set him off. Hence why she'd not told him she was leaving in the first place. She'd hoped to avoid the drama, except he'd somehow found her. He'd known to grab her at the airport. Proof that Darren's precious BBI had a leak. Or was it the message she'd sent to Sergei that led to Pierrot finding her?

Sergei wouldn't screw me. However, Sergei also wasn't happy with her. Was this his way of punishing her for not doing as told? Damn Darren for planting a seed of doubt.

"How did you know I was back in France?" she asked.

"I have my methods. You and I are more alike than you think. *Marina.*"

The fact that one of his men had used her Russian name was the only reason she had allowed them to bring her here—instead of killing them and disposing of their bodies. They'd confronted her, waylaying her just after customs, the big bald one saying, "Are you Marina Sokolov?" She'd wanted to shoot them on the spot for exposing her. But logic prevailed. Dead men couldn't answer questions.

Who'd sent them? Exactly how badly was her cover blown? Pierrot only ever knew her as Francesca, and she'd never known him to kidnap people before. Was this all a strange misunderstanding?

The first tactic she adopted? Ignorance. "I think you have me mistaken for someone else. My name is Francesca. Remember? You hired me."

He snorted. "You don't need to lie anymore. I know

you're one of Sergei's puppets. How do you think you came to work for me in the first place? He's used my fashion connections more than once to get his people somewhere he needed a job done."

Pierrot knew Sergei? The plot thickened. "Does he know you've kidnapped me?" Although it was less abduction and more her skipping along to see what the big, bad wolf wanted. "Answers before gutting," another of Kristoff's mottos.

"This is none of Sergei's business. I have other uses for you."

A disturbing declaration. "Whatever you're planning will have to wait. I'm in service to someone else." Someone currently alone and unprotected. She could only trust that Darren would manage to stay alive long enough for her to extricate herself and find him.

"You're here on a job in *my* city, yet you didn't even think to ask for permission." Pierrot made a sound and shook his head. "Such poor manners."

"I've never needed permission before."

"Things have changed."

No, the only thing that had changed was the size of Pierrot's ego. "Who told you I was coming?"

"I have my sources."

"I hope your source has their affairs in order." Because Marina wasn't a forgiving person. She still hadn't forgiven herself for ditching Darren.

"Threats? You seem to forget who has the upper hand."

Nothing to forget. As usual, a man chose to think having a dick made him superior. He'd soon realize how wrong that was. "What do you want?" Marina asked.

"For starters, I want an apology for screwing up my show."

Men and their vanity. She muttered something rude in Russian before snapping, "I'm sorry I stepped on your ego by not wearing your ugly creations for rich people who wouldn't know good taste if it slapped them." Apologizing wasn't her strong suit.

"You dare insult my vision?"

"Someone should. Your designs are ugly."

"Why, you rotten b—"

There was a commotion outside Pierrot's office and a brisk knock.

"*Je suis occupé!*" yelled her old runway boss.

"*I'm busy,*" *he says. Hmph.* More like being a pain in her derriere.

"*Nous avons attrapé quelqu'un...*"

Who did they catch? She listened to Pierrot and his man jabbering about a suspicious American male casing the place and thought, *No, he can't be that stupid. I told him if we were separated to go someplace safe.*

Except Darren *was* that dumb, and obviously possessed a hero complex. One could only hope he'd arrived with a weapon and a plan.

It wasn't long before Darren stumbled into the room, aided by a shove. He offered her a sheepish grin. "Hey, Fran."

Arms crossed over his chest, Pierrot sneered, "*Qui est-ce?*"

"This is my ex-boyfriend. It seems he is having problems letting go. Kind of like someone else around here."

"Don't make me out to be the bad guy," Darren snapped. "Why not explain what you did?"

"I dumped him." Her tone soft, as if confiding with Pierrot. "He couldn't handle it. Follows me around wherever I go."

"And you haven't killed him?" The Frenchman inhaled the drama with wide eyes. The French, always so emotional about things.

She shrugged. "What can I say? The sex was good. It seems a shame to murder him."

"Murder me? You did that when you left me without a word. Stabbed me right through the heart, she did." Darren played the role of jilted lover well. Too well.

"You were the one who made that big fuss when she fled?" Pierrot's brows arched. "*Il est fou de toi*. Idiot."

Marina shrugged. "*Il est amoureux de moi*." Darren loved her—once upon a time—and it touched something inside her to know he'd once cared enough to notice she was gone. It also warmed her to know he still gave enough of a damn to follow her here. That warmth was also tinged in anger that he'd put himself in danger.

Pierrot eyed him. "You don't speak French."

"Probably on account that I'm American."

"That explains your lack of manners," Pierrot said with a sneer.

"My manners? How about yours? I'd like to know what you're doing with Fran. I saw your guys kidnapping her."

"I would never kidnap. That would be a crime.

What you saw was merely my staff escorting her to a meeting with me."

"And now, I'm escorting her out. She and I need to talk." Darren faced off against Pierrot, who dropped his jovial demeanor.

"You are intruding on my business."

"Does your business always consist of strong-arming women?"

"I have not done a thing to Francesca, and your questions are annoying. As you can see, she is fine, and we have much to discuss. Alone," Pierrot emphasized. "Leave."

"Only if she comes with me." Darren's gaze held a stubborn hint. He wouldn't budge, and Marina held in a sigh. He would issue an ultimatum. That wouldn't go over well with the high-strung and temperamental Frenchman.

Pierrot drew himself as tall as his five-foot-five could go. "You are not in charge here. I am, and I say Francesca stays, and you will go."

"Like fuck." Darren crossed his arms, putting on his alpha face and tone.

Worst thing he could have done.

Pierrot spat, "I am done dealing with you. *Disposez de le cretin*." He waved a hand, and the thugs moved to grip Darren's arms.

Which meant it was time to act.

Marina, who Pierrot had stupidly left untied, whirled, her heel whipping up and around to clock the bald thug in the jaw, sending him staggering. The second guy never got a grip on Darren because he ducked out of it and threw a punch into the guy's gut. It wasn't enough to take down the bald brute, so she jabbed him in the face, breaking his nose, then clapped both his ears, to make them ring, before grabbing him and kneeing him hard in the balls.

Darren uttered a sympathetic male "Ouch."

Click. The sound of a safety being flipped off was loud, and Marina turned to see a gun pointed at them.

Pierrot scowled. "Women. Always causing me trouble, and they wonder why I prefer men. I've had enough of you both. Hands over your heads."

As if she'd listen. Only victims gave up against one player. Pierrot had a gun. But she had something better.

Surprise.

She whirled, facing Darren, and exclaimed, "One last kiss before we die." Then she plastered her mouth to his. He hesitated only a moment before crushing her mouth, slanting his lips over hers, and igniting a fire that had never gone out.

"Stop that," Pierrot demanded.

Instead, she added tongue. Darren got right into it, his hands groping her ass.

A weird thing happened when people kissed. Some people got turned on and stared—to the point they sometimes got horny and diddled themselves.

Others turned away from public displays of affection in disgust.

Two different reactions, yet there was one thing in common in both cases: they didn't act.

Which was how she turned a hot, panting kiss into the distraction she needed to whirl around and shove

Pierrot's gun arm to the side, trip him with a foot sweep behind the ankles, and land atop him, her knee pinning his chest.

Only then did she smile. "Now who's got the upper hand?"

CHAPTER FOURTEEN

THE KISS WAS EVERYTHING DARREN REMEMBERED. Hot. Sweet. Cock-hardening.

And a ploy. Marina used the embrace as a tactic to take down the short Frenchman holding them at gunpoint.

I feel so used—and frustrated. Was it wrong that he wanted to ignore the danger and kiss her some more?

Apparently, she didn't feel the same way.

"Grab his gun," she ordered as she held the man pinned down.

Why don't you grab me? A good retort, but shitty plan, given one of the thugs on the floor groaned. A weapon might come in handy in case their assailants hadn't learned their lesson.

Leaning over, he wrapped his hand around the solid grip of the weapon. He aimed it. While not a fan of firearms per se, he was no stranger to them. He pointed it at the Frenchman and said, "Talk."

Instead, Pierrot sputtered, "You can't do this to me."

Marina flicked him on the forehead. "Actually, Pierrot, I can."

"Do you know who I am? I am—"

She cut him off. "An annoying prick. You're also the guy who's going to start talking if he wants to live to design more ugly clothes. I've reached the limits of my patience with you. I want to know who tipped you off. Who told you about me arriving at the airport?"

"I will tell you nothing."

That made her tsk. "Why must you compound your initial stupidity in coming after me with even dumber choices like holding your tongue?" She pressed down on his neck, making Pierrot gasp for air. When she eased up, the Frenchman still thought he could argue.

"You will pay for this."

"For what? I haven't broken anything yet. Shall we rectify that?" She lifted her fist, and Pierrot screamed. Loudly. Emasculating all mankind in that moment.

Marina shook her head. "I haven't even hit you yet. Are you that much of a coward? How did you ever end up running a gang in this town?"

"Money can buy a lot of things, even false respect," Darren said.

"He should have used some of his wealth to buy common sense." She grabbed Pierrot by the ears and slammed his head a few times against the floor. "Let's try this again. Who." *Wham*. "Tipped." *Thunk*. "You off?"

Pierrot chose to spit. "*Mange moi, putain. Je vais te tuer.*"

"Kill me?" Marina laughed. "You and what army, little man?" Moving her legs, Marina pinned Pierrot's arms, straddling him almost intimately. All the better to torture him.

Marina leaned down close, really close. "You should have talked when you had the chance. You leave me no choice now. Shoot him," she said to Darren.

"If I shoot, you'll end up wearing spatter." Not to mention, it would cause problems. Unsanctioned kills in other countries never went over well, even if those people attempted to hurt him first.

"Good point. Do you have a shower here?" she asked Pierrot. "What about clothes? And not that weird shit you like to design."

"You won't shoot me." Pierrot tried to sound confident, but his voice shook.

"Then you obviously don't know me as well as you think you do." She smiled, that of a barracuda going after a little fish. "Keep refusing to answer and see what happens when you don't cooperate. I promise I can be quite innovative."

The man's complexion grew even paler. "This is quite unnecessary."

"Unnecessary was you abducting me and threatening my client."

"Your client? I thought he was your boyfriend." Pierrot's forehead knit, the furrows deep.

"Ex-boyfriend," she corrected. The emphasis bothered Darren. "Right now, he's the boss, which means I can't let you hurt him."

"You can't harm me either." Pierrot seemed quite certain. "I have friends. I am a man of importance."

Leaning low, Marina whispered, softly, sweetly. "I could wrap you in weights right now and drop you in the Seine. No one would know I did it. They might not ever find your body. And even if they did, once the fish eat your flesh..."

The whites of Pierrot's eyes popped, and Darren was surprised he managed to keep the orbs in his head.

"You wouldn't dare."

"I am getting mighty tired of people underestimating me. Darren, see if you can find some rope."

"Don't kill me." A high fluting thread of panic laced Pierrot's words.

"Then tell me what I want to know. Who notified you I was coming?"

"It was an anonymous tip."

A heavy breath blew out of Marina. "How convenient. Darren, the rope."

"How about a belt?" he said, hands going to his waist.

"I swear, it's the truth," Pierrot blubbered. "I got an email."

"What did it say? Did someone hire you to grab me?"

Now that fear had broken through the wall of his blustery courage, Pierrot couldn't spill his guts fast enough. "It wasn't a job. The message simply said a person of interest was arriving on a certain flight from the United States. As soon as I saw your face via the bodycam on my man, Lem, I knew it had to be you."

Or had the tipster meant Darren? Didn't matter. Their cover was blown, and they weren't even a day in Paris.

Marina made a noise. "So much for our plan to get here and bait our target. Now, will you believe me when I say it's your precious Bad Boy Inc. leaking our location?" She glared at Darren.

He stubbornly shook his head. "Don't blame this on me. I doubt Harry knows Pierrot, your old modeling boss, moonlights as a wannabe mafia lord."

Marina turned back to Pierrot. "Anything else? Did you trace the email? Anything?"

A violent shake of his head. "No."

Which left them no further ahead.

"Think it was the island mastermind?" Darren asked. A person who'd become a real thorn in Darren's side. He already had reason to believe they were behind the assassination attempts and the island fiasco. But whoever the shadowy figure was, they were doing more than just attacking operatives and pitting them against each other. The faceless enemy was seeding gangs in cities. Drug gangs. Money laundering. Darren had reports from around the globe of mysterious figures running things behind the scenes as crime ramped up.

BBI had recently busted one of those rings. Calvin, a top student from the academy, had helped bring it down. Reaper had run into trouble, too, as someone thought it funny to pit a hitman and hitwoman against each other. Other agencies Darren knew of claimed they'd been hit, as well.

Why? Why attack so many of them at once?

A vendetta of this size was unusual. Typically revenge involved one person, one entity, not a whole group. Which led to the second, more likely possibility: instability. Why destabilize mercenary groups unless... *Someone is planning a coup.* And they didn't want any outside help interfering.

"Could be Mastermind, but how is he so well-informed? We shouldn't have been traced so quickly."

Unless they'd been betrayed. He didn't say it aloud this time. He didn't have to because they both could see the truth, just not the culprit. Was her precious Sergei and his office to blame? Or did a mole exist at BBI? At this point, it was crucial that they find out one way or the other.

"We need to make new plans," she stated, rising from Pierrot's chest.

"The kind we don't tell anyone about?" Darren arched a brow.

"Do we have enough funds to go dark?" Marina asked.

"More than enough." Darren might not be the trained killer Marina was, but he had his uses.

At the mention of funds, Pierrot brightened, his fear quickly evaporating at the prospect of making money. "I will help, for a price."

"I don't need help." Flatly spoken by Marina.

The Frenchman sneered. "Says the woman so easily caught."

"You foolish little man. Have you not yet grasped that I let them catch me? How else to find out who my enemy is? And even better, you had me brought to your

HITMAN WEDDING • 149

headquarters. I guess I should thank you for giving me access to everything I need." With that statement, she soundly hog-tied Pierrot and his henchmen before proceeding to ransack his office, pulling out guns, plastic ties, and money. Lots of it.

She stuffed it into a bag, along with the weapons.

Darren shook his head. "You know I wasn't kidding when I said I could get my hands on some cash."

"I know." She tossed him a look as she armed herself under her jacket. "But I'm going to wager any of those methods will leave some kind of trail. This"—she jabbed a finger at the bundle of banknotes peeking out of the bag—"won't. Let's go."

"What about these guys?" Darren pointed to Pierrot, who glared at them but couldn't speak past the crumpled paper shoved into his mouth.

"What about them? I'm sure someone will come along and free them. Eventually." She dropped to her haunches. "And if Pierrot is smart, he'll stay far, far away from me because, next time, I won't be so nice."

With that threat, she stood and walked out, tall, gorgeous, and deadly. Darren couldn't help but want her.

He ignored the thugs on the floor and went after Marina. He caught up to her outside the office in a room that seemed to have many purposes, from sorting packages of what looked to be a table full of bricks wrapped in plastic—most likely drugs—to pallets with boxes strapped to them. "Since we've ditched our current plan, any thoughts on what we should do next?"

"You're the one who wanted to come to Paris because of a tip."

Actually, Harry had suggested Greece, but Darren wanted Paris. A perverse kind of torture, for him at least.

"We're here because Declan has been digging around."

"Who is Declan?" she asked, flicking him a glance over her shoulder.

"Academy graduate in advanced technologies."

"A hacker."

"Yes, a hacker. He managed to trace some of the orders for the island—food, flowers, even staff—to a place outside the city."

"He found a trail?" She sounded surprised.

"More than likely a false one, but something we can look into."

"You have an address?"

"Yes."

"We'll go there. It keeps us moving at the very least."

"Now?"

"You have something better to do?" she asked with an arched brow.

"A shower, shave, and some food comes to mind."

She uttered a heavy sigh. "If we must."

"Yes, we must. We have to refuel at some point."

"I know a safe place you can go while I check out this clue."

He shook his head. "Like fuck are you stuffing me in some safe prison while you go gallivanting off. I go

where you go. Unless you're planning to tie me up, too."
He meant it as a joke.

She took him quite literally. "That's not a bad idea."

"I'm your client. You can't restrain me."

"I can if I think it's necessary. But don't worry, there's no extra charge for it." She winked. When she approached him, he took a wary step back, and she laughed. "So skittish. I was going to grab your suitcase. Or were you planning to leave it behind?"

He noted it behind him and felt stupid. What had he thought she'd do?

As if reading his mind, she said, "Did you really think I'd tie you up here? You're much too heavy to carry."

"Was that another dig about my weight?" Darren worked hard to remain fit, yet he was getting to be of an age where he should be more careful.

"I'm sure you work out as often as your job allows." The words trailed behind her as she left the storage room, and he hurried behind. Always following.

They entered a garage area where she startled a man wiping down the car used to kidnap her. "Do you have the keys?" she said without preamble.

The man frowned. "Where're Lem and Benoit?"

"Is that a yes or a no?" she asked as she neared the guy.

"*Eh, Benoit, que est-ce—*"

Whack. She punched him in the nose, and the guy grabbed his face, screaming. The sound was cut short when she clocked him again on the temple. He dropped like a sack of rocks. She rifled through his pockets.

Darren resumed their conversation. "I am not fat."

Turning her head to look at him and dangling the keys she'd found, Marina snorted. "If you say so, tubby."

"I'll show you tubby," he growled, stalking toward her.

"You're right. We will see when you get in the car. Hopefully, we won't have to drive on two wheels."

That kind of comment was why, after he tucked his luggage into the trunk with hers, he sat gingerly in the small vehicle. Being a wretched wench, she laughed as she hopped into the driver seat. "Your face. So priceless," she snickered.

"Now where?" he grumbled.

"Do you have the address of the place your Declan found?"

"Yeah." He'd memorized it. He gave it to her, yet she punched in something else.

"What's that?" He jabbed a finger at the screen as she approached the loading doors to the warehouse.

"Basic rule of using a GPS on a car you've stolen. Never enter your true location."

The rebuke brought a wince. Subterfuge obviously wasn't his strength.

When she pulled out her phone, he snatched it from her hand.

"What are you doing?" she asked. "Give it back. I need to call Sergei."

"Nope. Not happening." He rolled down his window and pitched the phone. He then tossed his after it.

"You idiot. Now how are we supposed to get any field support?"

"We've got money and brains. We don't need anyone."

"Says you."

"Yeah, says me. No calling anyone for the next little bit, not until we know who is betraying us on the inside."

"Sergei wouldn't do that."

"Neither would Harry."

"I don't like you."

She said it first this time.

"Too bad," was his reply.

A red light meant they were stopped and could glare at each other. The tension between them was taut. Ripe with expectation. He couldn't help but remember the kiss. That stupid, sizzling embrace that made him feel things. The same feelings he had when he kissed Fran. Except now, he knew there was no Fran, only Marina, yet it didn't change the attraction.

He broke the eye contact first, turning his head and uttering a brusque, "I meant what I said before. We should find a place to crash for the night."

"I'm not tired. I can drive. But first, we need to change cars. They'll be looking for this one." She stopped the car and motioned for him to get out. They were still within the warehouse district, which meant little light and even fewer prying eyes.

He exited and grabbed the luggage from the trunk then waited as she bent down and did something under the steering wheel before exiting herself. As she strutted away, he joined her, trailing the two damned suitcases behind him like a servant, wondering how far they'd have to walk before finding a new ride.

A whoosh from behind startled, and he peered over his shoulder to see the car on fire.

"That should muddy our trail a bit," she said as she tried the doors on cars parked by the sidewalk.

"We're stealing another car?"

"Borrowing," she stated as the third vehicle bore fruit. "But we won't be taking it far."

They took it only as far as a main road, where they ditched it, intact, and caught a taxi, which deposited them at a seedy hotel on the outskirts of the capital. The kind that didn't ask questions and kept no records when paid in cash.

The one thing she did that he thought odd was asking for a single room.

"Only one?" he asked when they'd reached their floor—the fifth level, and via an elevator that creaked and groaned.

"It will be easier to protect you if I'm close."

She opened the door and went in first, checking out every nook and cranny, peeking in the bathroom and even out the window before kicking off her shoes.

Given that Darren would probably get billed somehow for this hotel—despite the fact that the money she'd used was stolen—he felt no qualms about throwing himself on the coverlet and declaring, "Mine."

What he didn't expect was for her to land atop him stating, "Share."

CHAPTER FIFTEEN

"What are you doing?"

"You were the one who said we needed to rest," Marina said.

"Then you should have gotten two beds."

"Seems like a waste when we can share this one." She wiggled atop him, meaning to fluster him, and it worked. His cheeks took on a ruddy color, and his gaze smoldered. What she didn't expect was to get flustered herself.

Don't lie. She'd known what to expect. The kiss had given her ample warning. It had ignited the simmering passion that he always managed to evoke. For all she kept saying she'd used him, exploited his body, abused his trusting nature, she'd enjoyed it. Enjoyed him.

I miss him. Miss what we had.

"Get off me." Spoken through gritted teeth, Darren glared.

Perhaps, had he reacted favorably to her presence,

she might have backed off, but this stubbornness of his, this insistence that he didn't want her, she didn't like it. Especially since the hardness pressing against her told the real truth. "Feels more like you should be saying 'get me off.'"

"I am not having sex with you."

"Why not?"

"I told you. I don't sleep with my employees."

The rule made her roll her eyes. "You and your morals."

"Don't mock my ethics. At least I have some."

"And they're cute, if misplaced. But since you are so adamant about it, for the next hour, I won't be in your employ."

"What's that supposed to mean?"

"It means, I will tell Sergei not to bill you. Right now, we are just a man and a woman in the same room, wearing too many clothes. I say we do something about that."

"No."

"No, it won't take an hour?" She gyrated again, noting how his nostrils flared. "I agree. Probably ten minutes, tops. Although, we might be able to extend that with a bit of foreplay."

"This isn't amusing."

"You're right. It's not. I am aroused, and you are doing nothing about it." Usually, by now, she'd be flat on her back with her legs on his shoulders as he entered her.

"Don't you see how wrong this is?"

"Not really. You are attracted to me, and I am

attracted to you. We should be adults about it and have sex."

"That isn't a solution."

"Why not? You know it will feel good." She punctuated that claim with a tug on his lower lip.

He turned his head, freeing himself. "What if I don't want casual sex?"

"You had no problem before. As I recall, all we did was have sex."

"We did more than that," he retorted.

She looked him dead in the eyes. "Are you going to claim that we talked and spent hours going on dates and other things couples do?" She arched a brow. "You can't because we rarely left the apartment, and when we did, it was only to grab food so that we had energy for more sex. You never really tried to get to know me. Never even made it to one of my photo shoots."

"I didn't want to disturb you while you were working."

"You don't have to lie. It was obvious you weren't interested in me as a person."

"Well, that person was fake."

"That isn't the point. You might have realized that had you spent more time getting me to talk rather than blowing your cock."

"You are vulgar."

"And you're a hypocrite."

"How am I a hypocrite for not wanting you to use me as a dildo to get off?"

"Because, when you thought I was some vapid model, you had no problem using me."

His lips flattened. "I'm sorry."

"I'll forgive you"—she lowered her voice to a husky whisper—"if you do that thing with your tongue."

Rather than bury his face between her legs, he shoved at her.

Or tried to. Marina held on to him, enjoying how he bucked and heaved, but didn't hurt. Even now, frustrated and angry, Darren didn't lift a hand to hurt her.

It made stripping him so much fun.

He yelled, "Stop it." His hands grabbed for hers.

She evaded them and laughed as she said, "Make me."

The wrestling involved much ripping of clothes, popping of buttons until he was clad in only his boxer briefs. She stood in triumph, lips curved into a satisfied smirk. "That's better."

"You're insane," he growled, sounding angry, yet he couldn't hide his erection. The front of his shorts tented, but it was his smoldering gaze that promised the pleasure to come.

About time.

She stripped off her shirt and let it hit the floor. He stared at her. She unbuttoned her pants next, shoving them down and kicking them away, leaving her clad in only her underpants and a bra.

He rose from the bed, stood staring. Hungry.

She understood that emotion. She crooked a finger at him.

He hesitated, and she got to watch his inner battle. Morals lost to need. He dove at her, his big body slamming into hers, pushing her back until she hit the wall hard enough that she gasped.

This was the passion she'd missed. The man she couldn't stop craving.

He leaned his heavy body against her, and his lips found the soft curve of her neck. He nibbled and sucked, teasing her sensitive spots, knowing her body and how to please her. She couldn't help but run her fingers through his short, thick hair, her head arched back to give him unhindered access to her flesh.

He didn't kiss her lips. Didn't say a word as he trailed a fiery path down her neck then lower still until he nuzzled the valley between her breasts. His hot breath steamed her skin. The rough bristles on his jaw scraped.

She trembled in anticipation as his mouth brushed over the fabric of her bra. He nipped at her nipple before sucking it through the material, drawing a groan from her as he teased. He drew most of her breast into his mouth, frustrating her because she wanted to feel his mouth on her skin.

"Take it off," she demanded.

"Don't tell me what to do," he growled against her, the sound vibrating her flesh.

He bit the tip, and she cried out, arching away from the wall, pushing into him. Then, since he wouldn't remove the bra, she reached behind to fumble with the clasp, but it refused to cooperate, and she made a sound of frustration.

"Impatient?" he teased, but at the same time, he

pushed her hands away, and she heard a rip as he tore the offending thing from her.

The air of the room kissed her newly bared breasts, still damp from his sucking. Quivering with anticipation. He didn't disappoint, latching onto her nipple, sucking it, pulling it into his mouth, the hard tugs sending an exciting jolt to her sex.

He swapped breasts, giving the other the same attention, making her moan and tremble as her body reacted to his touch.

When he dropped to his knees, she held her breath. She knew what to expect.

Craved the pleasure he would give.

But he teased her first, nuzzling the soft flesh of her belly. He took his sweet time, pressing kisses against her, his hands gripping her thighs. He rubbed his face against her mound, the thin fabric of her panties barely a barrier.

Could he tell how wet she was for him? How much she ached?

His hands pushed at her legs, and she eagerly parted them to give him access. He pressed kisses against her, the panties in the way of his lips, and still she moaned, her fingers clutching at his head, urging him to do more.

She even pushed her pelvis forward, a silent invitation, but he wanted to tease. He kissed her inner thigh. Soft, light caresses.

She released his hair to tug at her panties, and he laughed against her skin, making her shiver.

"You're awfully impatient."

"I'm going to finish without you if you don't hurry

up," she grumbled as her panties hit the floor and she stepped out of them.

"But your body is like a fine wine," he said, rubbing his rough cheek on her thigh. "It should be savored."

"Then savor it, dammit." She grabbed his hair and pushed his face against her. She expected him to fight, but instead, he went willingly, burying his face between her legs as he ran a long, wet lick against her sex. She sighed. Then cried out as he parted her nether lips and let his tongue stab her. He lapped and then flicked her nub, skimmed and licked, over and over again, giving her what she craved.

"Yes," she hissed as she rocked against his face. Pleasure built inside her, fast and familiar. She let it fill her up. He clamped his lips down on her clitoris, tugging it, and she cried out as her climax hit. The waves of her orgasm rippled through her channel, fun but so much better when she had something to grip.

"Fuck me," she demanded. "I want to feel you inside me, now."

He didn't argue. Rather he stood, dropped his boxers then gripped her leg, pulling it up and around his hip, angling her body in a way that exposed her to him. He plunged into her, his long and thick shaft big and familiar, filling her up so perfectly. She clung to him and panted as he thrust. Made soft moaning sounds as he pumped into her, his hard cock a mighty piston that was exactly what the ebbing waves of her orgasm craved.

Her pleasure began to coil again, a spring that wound itself tighter and tighter. He had to push and pull with each stroke, the suction of her body not wanting to let him go.

She couldn't have said who started the kiss, only that it happened. Their lips clashed, and she tasted herself on him. And liked it. The aroma of her arousal an unnecessary aphrodisiac. She clung to him as he kept pumping, his strokes hitting her at just the right angle, just the right spot.

The muscles in her channel tightened. Her body tensed. The need in her coiled. Her sex clung to his cock, squeezing him as he tipped deep, pushing against her. Pulsing inside her.

When she climaxed the second time, she did so loudly, the scream ragged and high-pitched. She didn't hide it or hold it in. His fingers dug into her flesh as he drove hard and deep one last time.

Their passion spent, they staggered to the bed where they lay panting, their skin dewy on the sheets. The sex as incredible as ever. Maybe even better because she could be herself.

They slept, wrapped around each other, which led to early morning sex. Sex in the shower. Only the lure of food dragging them from the room and into reality. When he offered to go get them coffee and donuts, she agreed, watching from the window until she saw him cross the street. Then, using the clunky phone in the room, she entered a series of numbers, a string of digits she'd memorized a while ago for use in case of emergency.

The phone was answered, and no one spoke. She recited a stream of letters and digits, a code that indicated her identity and that it was safe to speak. Then she gushed quickly in Russian, "I am with Darren. We were ambushed last night, so we've gone off-grid."

"Whose idea was that? And what have you done to your chip? It's not broadcasting your signal. It hasn't uttered a single blip since you escaped the island. And don't tell me it's because of the water again. You're not anywhere near water."

"I think it got wrecked from a bullet that skimmed me." The furrow on her arm had scabbed and only throbbed a little when she soaped it.

"And you just thought to tell me now?"

"Forget the chip. I only called to let you know I'm still with Darren. We're going to visit someplace outside the city."

"Where?"

She told him.

Sergei whistled. "That's a few hours out of town."

"Think of it as racking up billable hours."

"Is that bill going to get paid?"

"What's that supposed to mean?"

"You're soft for him." Sergei didn't bark it. He didn't sound mad at all, which worried her.

"I feel nothing for him."

"I think you lie. Perhaps you should come home and let someone else take care of him. Someone more objective."

"I can do my job."

"Can you? I guess we'll soon see."

She hung up the phone and watched as Darren jogged back across the street. Sergei would kill her if he knew she'd let Darren out of her sight. What was she thinking? She had a job to do, and fucking Darren wasn't part of it.

Yet that didn't stop her from grabbing him the moment he walked through the door and riding him hard a few minutes later, eyes closed against the future, living only for the pleasure of the present. Pretending tomorrow would never come.

CHAPTER SIXTEEN

THE MORNING HAD A SURREAL FEEL TO IT. ON THE one hand—which rested quite comfortably on her boob —being with Fran/Marina, her limbs wrapped around him, was like a familiar sweater, the kind that knew how to make your world comfortable and right. At the same time, having her beside him, naked, her skin as soft as he remembered, caused a tense excitement. This wasn't the same woman he used to know. Forget soft and docile, this female was ferocious.

The secrets between them had unraveled. He saw her now for the first time, and she saw him. If he were to be honest, he would admit that he'd also hidden his true self from Fran. The Darren that Fran had dated for those few weeks was a suit-wearing businessman. He carried around a laptop. Had a personal manservant named Marcus. He'd neglected to mention at the time that Marcus had more duties than picking up his laundry and taking messages.

At no time did he find himself tempted to admit to Fran that he ran an academy for misfits he turned into elite soldiers for hire. The Fran he'd fucked in Paris what seemed like a lifetime ago would have gasped and run from the violence he essentially condoned every single day.

Marina, on the other hand, embraced his lifestyle. There would be no judgment from her. Violence and firm methods for getting the job done wouldn't shock or frighten her. Hell, given her fearlessness, Marina would probably want to be a part of the mayhem. She was utterly nuts. Beautiful. The perfect partner for a man like him who ran in interesting circles.

She was also a perfect liar. He saw how good she was when he returned from getting them breakfast.

"Did you miss me while I was gone?" he asked and watched her face.

She wore the remnants of his dress shirt, the buttons popped, meaning the linen gaped open, flashing flesh. Panties on her bottom half, which only served to tease his view.

"You took too long."

He held up the tray with coffees and the bag with treats. "They had just finished making some croissants. They made me wait while they cooled down."

"Give me." She held out a hand, and he passed the bag over.

She almost bounced away from him, her excitement for a pastry quite palpable. She perched on the bed, crossing her legs. He might have enjoyed an interesting view if not for those pink cotton panties.

The croissant hit her lips, her head tipped back, and she groaned. Moaned in such a way that she almost found herself mauled.

He restrained himself and took the only seat in the room. He sipped his coffee as he perused her.

She'd eaten the entire first croissant, unabashedly stuffing it into her mouth, humming happily. This woman was a liar. Quite possibly his enemy. How dare she look so fucking hot it hurt?

Time to remind himself that they might not be working for the same outcome. "How is Sergei?"

Her shoulders rolled. "Fine. I guess. I didn't ask."

"Not going to deny you called him?"

She raised her gaze. "You're not stupid. You left me alone with a phone. You had to know I'd call someone."

"And what did you chat about?"

"I let him know I was secure."

"I'm sure you said more than that. What did he say to you?"

"You really want to know?" She fixed him with a look. "He wanted to remind me not to get distracted and to do my job."

I saw no signs of distraction during the blowjob. He crossed his legs as his mind played in colorful detail said bj from their shower. "If you don't want to fuck again, you can just say so." He didn't need her using Sergei as an excuse to skip sex.

"Is this where I remind you of your own rule? You know, the one where you don't have sex with your employees."

"Are you working for me again?"

"I am most definitely back on the job now that I'm cured of my distraction."

He didn't know if he should be flattered that he made her thought process wonky or annoyed she'd used him and now had no reason for him other than a paycheck.

"So that's it, then? Just like that, we're back to business only."

"I'm glad you understand."

"I hope this means you won't be clingy," he muttered.

"I am never clingy, and I wouldn't recommend you try," she said, wagging her finger at him.

"You were the one who used to be glued to me when I was trying to work."

"That was Fran. Fran cuddles."

"And what does Marina do?" he asked, taking a sip of his coffee.

"Marina sits on the couch alone to watch television, and if she needs sex, she spreads her legs and masturbates until you come over."

He spat out his coffee to her laughter.

"You are such a man," she snickered.

"You're doing this on purpose to be shocking. Why?" he asked, using a napkin to wipe the hopeless coffee spots on his pants.

"Because I can. I enjoy watching your reactions."

"You're intentionally trying to make me dislike you."

"Is it working?"

No. "I don't have to like or dislike you to work with you. What I do need is a measure of trust. How am I supposed to trust you when you keep running to Sergei?" In a fight, could he trust her to have his back? Or would she stick a knife in it?

"He wouldn't betray me."

"You going to tell me he is like a father?"

"No." Her nose wrinkled. "My father and mother left me. Sergei is my handler. We are a team. If I fail, he doesn't get paid. Sergei would never do anything to jeopardize his paycheck."

"Unless someone made him a better offer."

"He wouldn't do that." Spoken with conviction, but Darren wasn't as certain. He'd seen the depravity of mankind. Had played a part in some of its downfall, too.

"If you're so certain about Sergei and his team, then you won't mind a little bet. A head-to-head battle, so to speak. If my guys are the leak, you win. If it's Sergei, then I do."

"What are we wagering?" she asked before taking another bite of her third croissant, this one covered in icing sugar. A dessert for breakfast.

"I guess we need a prize," he said. "What do you want?" He was looking at it. One night in her arms, and buried to the hilt in her body just wasn't enough. He needed more.

But she didn't ask him to bury his face between her thighs. "I want a favor later on."

That brought a furrow to his brow. "A favor? What kind of favor?"

At the query, she rolled her shoulders. "I don't know yet. But one day, I will call you and cash in."

"Seems pretty broad. What if you want me to kill someone or something?"

"I didn't take you for a pussy."

"Bravery has nothing to do with murder." He didn't believe in killing people without just cause.

"What if I promise it won't require you to kill anyone?"

"No genie wishes," he added.

"What's a genie wish?"

"The vague one that is 'save my family from ruin,' only it requires me ruining myself to save it."

"You're making this very complicated. Are you that convinced you'll lose?" Marina smirked as she trapped him.

He trusted Harry. Could he 100 percent trust his team? "Fine. If you win, you get a favor."

"Excellent." She clapped her hands.

"Aren't you going to ask me what I want?"

"Why bother? You are going to lose." She offered him a cocky smile.

Perhaps that was why he did it. Why he said it. "If I win, you have to live with me for a month."

It took her a moment, her mouth rounded in surprise, her eyes wide. Then she laughed. "You can't be serious."

"Totally. If Sergei is the rat, you, Marina Francesca Sokolov, are going to become my temporary live-in girlfriend."

"Being Fran for a whole month seems like unnecessarily cruel punishment," she noted.

"What if I said I don't want Fran, but Marina?"

For a moment, she blinked at him, and he kind of wanted to take the words back. Had he lost his balls? Spilling a stupidly girly sentiment like that to her face!

"Agreed." She reached out, and he hesitated a second in shock.

Holy shit. She was gonna live with him for a month if he won. He extended his hand for a shake, sealing the pact. The pressure was on. *I'd better fucking win.* "During that month, no running off on odd jobs," he stated.

"Sure. I'll even fuck you and play nice if we have to do public functions."

"You're being awfully amenable. Is this your way of saying you like me?"

"No, it's my way of saying it won't happen. I am going to win the bet. Although your choice is odd. I would have thought you'd ask for a free job. Say like bodyguarding for a year or something."

"You would have agreed?"

"Yes, because you're going to lose." With that, she bounced off the bed and rummaged through her small suitcase. She outfitted herself in black yoga pants and a cowled, dark gray sweater.

Is she my enemy or not? He'd slept with her and still didn't know the answer. Good news, though. She hadn't killed him in his sleep. Then again, knowing her, she'd want to do it face-to-face.

She slid the gun she'd filched from Pierrot into the waistband at her back, using an academy trick where she twisted the elastic of her thong around the grip to keep it from sliding around. She tucked her sweater over it before putting on a dark jean jacket.

Darren asked, "Did you tell Sergei where we were going?"

She shook her head but didn't look him in the eyes.

She's lying.

"Did you tell your crew?" She bent to tie her shoes.

"Nope. So we shouldn't be running into anyone where we're headed. Which, by the way, isn't quite where I told you."

"Explain."

"I'll be driving the next leg." He dangled keys at her.

"What are those?"

"I rented a car."

"How?" she asked. "You weren't gone that long."

"I popped by the registration desk, and the guy there knew a guy, and they took care of it for me."

"A rental will leave a trail."

"How else do you suggest we travel? And don't say steal a car."

She grumbled. "You shouldn't have done that without talking to me."

"Does that mean you're going to run everything by me before doing it?" At her glare, he laughed. "You're being silly. If I were Sergei, and I did this, you'd be kissing my ass."

"No, I wouldn't. It's very hairy."

That resulted in more spewed coffee, which was why he set the cup down and grabbed his suitcase. "It is not hairy. If you're done making me choke—"

"Because I am also a gifted conversationalist. It's on

my list of attributes," she interrupted. "If you are ready, we should go."

Always ready to go. But she meant onto the next leg of their trip and not back to bed.

"I've got everything, including the car keys." He dangled them. "Front desk says the car is parked out front."

"I can't believe you involved them," she muttered. "Way to stay under the radar."

"Still waiting for you to actually explain what your plan is. Because, as far as I can tell, all you did this morning was sit around in your underwear eating and yakking our secrets."

"Masturbated, too."

No coffee to spew that time. "Let's go. Your chariot awaits."

The door to their room needed no help slamming shut behind them.

"You'd better not mean a chariot for real or anything too flashy that will draw attention."

"I might not be Russian," he snapped as they hit the elevator, "but I am not a complete idiot. I didn't get anything stupid. I rented something very generic and paid cash."

"I guess we could switch the plates."

"There you go. Great idea. I'll handle that, if you can provide a distraction that keeps people from coming outside for a few minutes."

They exited into the lobby where no one paid them any mind. Darren had no idea what she planned to give him his distraction. He should have asked or set out a list of rules.

The next thing he knew, she punched him hard in the arm and exclaimed, in a heavy Russian accent, "You pig. With my sister!"

"What the fuck is wrong with you?" he yelled back as she hit him again.

"She told me what you did. In our house!" She grabbed a plastic sleeve with brochures from the desk—manned by a wide-eyed young man with piercings all over—and threw it.

He easily dodged it and ducked the pen she threw at him. She bent down to get her shoe, cursing him out in Russian while the attendant muttered an ineffectual and cautious, "Madame? *Pouvez-vous calmer—*"

Darren chose to duck outside rather than watch the act. He noted the rental, as described, parked at the curb, snug between cars. He popped the trunk first to slide in his suitcase then feigned dropping something. He used the Swiss army utility knife he'd found at Pierrot's—while she grabbed the bigger firepower weapons—to unscrew the bolts. He quickly swapped the plates with the car behind him. It took care of the back. He then went to the front, opening the hood before dropping down to change the other one. Done in under two minutes. No one seemed to take notice.

He hopped into the car and pulled out, heading toward the front door of the hotel where Marina exited, looking smug and holding a napkin.

"What's that?" he asked as he pulled out of the parking area.

"A phone number. A nice man inside said he would

never cheat on me like my pig rat boyfriend." She smiled.

"I would never cheat."

"What all men say. Actions speak louder."

How could he act when he wasn't even sure he wanted to get involved? Sleeping with Marina had just muddied the issue. "I'm not the one who went into our first relationship lying."

"Good thing we won't make that mistake again."

The statement made him tighten his grip on the wheel.

"Where are we going?" she asked.

"You'll see."

"Tell me."

"Annoying when someone else does it, isn't it?" Petty revenge for when she wouldn't answer? Yeah, and he was okay with it.

"You are making it impossible for me to be your bodyguard. It's a wonder you haven't died yet."

"Maybe that's because I don't trust a known Russian operative with all the little details."

"I am not the one trying to kill you."

"Not yet."

"If you think I'm a risk, then why not fire me?"

He flashed her a grin. "I live only once."

The reply took her aback, and it took a short moment before she chuckled. "You won't live long if you don't tell me where we're going."

"Nope. If you don't know, you can't leak it."

"Leak it to whom?" She flung out her hands. "You threw out my cellphone."

"I did, yet you still managed to call your handler. So, now, I guess we see how trustworthy he is because I am going to wager that you gave him the false address."

"I told you I didn't."

"I call bullshit."

Her lips pursed. "Maybe I told him."

"After I told you not to."

"How do I know you are not leading me into a trap? Someone needs to know where to look for my body."

"I don't want to kill you." Not anymore. Getting in her pants again, though... Totally different thing.

"This place we're going, who knows about it?"

"Harry and Mason, probably a few other Bad Boy agents. I had them scout it as well as they could online."

"Not in person."

"We didn't want to tip anyone off." Especially since whoever was behind the shenanigans on the island sent the orders from the school they were going to visit.

A school currently on fire. They saw the smoke from blocks away.

Parked at the curb, up the street, Darren gaped at it. The bright, flashing lights of emergency vehicles lit up the area, but brighter still the flames dancing from the carcass of the school, the smoke thick.

Not as thick as her smug grin. "And it looks like I win."

Because Sergei hadn't been told about this place.

Only Harry and his team knew.

"There must be a mistake."

"No mistake. You owe me a favor. *Loser*."

Except it turned out that they'd both lost. Because

the school wasn't the only building hit that night. The decoy location, the one Marina had told Sergei about was hit, too.

It could mean only one thing.

They were fucked.

CHAPTER SEVENTEEN

THE SOBERING RESULTS OF THEIR WAGER MEANT little was said between them. Using more of Pierrot's cash and fake names, they checked into a motel.

Darren said nothing as he entered the room and saw the single bed. Didn't make any overtures or touch her. Hell, he barely even looked at her.

It angered Marina and, at the same time, ignited need inside her. She wanted to be aloof, knowing theirs was a doomed pairing. Yet, her attraction to him was crazy.

She couldn't help it. Sergei was right to ask her if she was fit to get the job done. Because the real answer was... *I don't know.*

Darren made her forget things. Forget the rigid control she usually conducted herself with. He drove her wild.

Whereas he appeared to feel nothing. He had no problem putting the passion they shared aside.

Or so he made it seem. When she stripped, right down to her panties and a T-shirt she pulled from her suitcase, she caught him watching.

From the corner of his eye, he peeked. Then quickly turned away.

Perhaps he faked a lack of interest as hard as she did.

What would happen if she tested that?

She stalked toward him on bare feet. Silent, and yet, he didn't jump when she grabbed him from behind. She spun him, and he stared at her, his eyes smoldering, but still, he made no move.

Very well. She grabbed his cheeks and yanked him down. He didn't resist, and she kissed him. He kissed her back. Hands soon tugged clothing free, a zipper and button for him, her panties to her ankles for her. The passion, quick and furious, had her screaming in moments and him grunting right after.

How could this be wrong?

This isn't what I should be doing.

Their hearts had barely slowed when she was off the bed, angry energy coursing through her veins. She began cursing, a ranting in a mix of Russian, English, French, and some Italian, wearing her hot temper and nothing else.

Being a man, Darren stared. "You're gorgeous."

"I know."

"And athletic, too. I don't know how I didn't recognize that before. You're not just toned. That's real muscle. The kind that comes from more than regular workouts."

"I am a finely tuned fighting machine." She posed and flexed. "A weak agent can't defend themselves or their clients."

"How did I ever believe you were a soft-spoken French model?" He didn't say it with any heated anger. Just a half-smile and a shake of his head.

"You made assumptions. Most people do. You look at the face and the body"—she gestured to her frame —"but never past it. You liked being flattered. And the sex was good."

"The sex is incredible." The vehemence with which he said it almost made her blush.

"Now it is. Before, it was okay." Because she had to hide her hot-blooded passion behind a meek mask.

"Your idea of okay was still mind-blowing, which is why I blame you for not spotting the clues. Because of you, my poor brain rarely had enough blood to function."

The backwards compliment had her blinking.

He laughed. "Want to hear something crazy?"

Crazier than his admission?

"I like Marina more than Fran."

"You're lying." Even if she didn't see why he'd do so.

"I'm actually really glad you ditched me the way you did. I mean, let's be serious. The meek and mild-mannered model I fell for was never going to last. You were right; we never got to know each other outside the bedroom. Once the passion fizzled, I would have been bored with Fran. We had nothing in common."

"We still don't."

"Don't we?" He arched a brow. "We both lead double lives."

"You run a school. I run special operations."

"I understand your world, and you understand mine."

"Is this where you say it's a small world and start singing?"

"Just that fate is strange sometimes. I mean, look at the fact that we never even met."

"Why would we?"

"Because I keep tabs on some of the more active players in the mercenary world."

"Why? You have your own group to use."

"I do. BBI is my agency of choice; however, who do you think trains the students? I like keeping my finger in the pie because you never know when you'll want to recruit a new teacher. Yet, with all my intel, I've never heard of your Sergei or seen even a hint of you."

"Because we know how to hide our tracks."

"Is this your way of saying if I dig I won't find anything?"

Why would he dig? What was Darren up to with this conversation? "I don't understand your interest."

"I want to know more about you."

"There is no need for that. We're not dating."

"Is the idea of sharing something personal that hard for you to grasp?"

"What have you shared?" she retorted. "I've yet to hear you talk much about your childhood and secrets."

"I was an only child. My mother died young. Super young. Murdered, actually. She was the catalyst for my father starting the academy. Did you know," he said leaning forward, his expression intent, "I used to hate the school. I blamed it for so much when I was a kid."

"How can you blame a school for anything?"

He shrugged. "I was grieving. I'd lost my mother, and my father wallowed in his depression. When he finally got past his grief, he became consumed with the academy and getting his revenge."

"Is this a story of a poor little rich boy ignored by his daddy?"

"Who found his balls and got over it. I came to realize over the years that everyone handles grief differently."

"If you grieve, it's because you let someone get too close."

"Are you going to tell me they don't allow you to care for anyone?"

She didn't need to feel Sergei's ghostly breath to reply, "The job comes first."

"Speaking of job, since both our offices failed the trust litmus test, we need to try something new."

"I still don't believe Sergei betrayed me."

"Just like I don't think Harry did. What if it's not them? What if we're still dealing with the mastermind from the island? Think about it. We weren't attacked at the hotel."

"Because we told no one where we were."

"Exactly. The only thing kind of public was our probable destination."

"You think our offices have a hack?"

"It would make sense. I know Declan is a whiz when it comes to cracking shit."

"Let's say you're right and someone is playing us both because they've managed to infiltrate our networks. How do we stop it? Short of crushing the computers and starting from scratch, which we both know isn't feasible."

"Declan might be able to find the hole."

"Isn't Declan the same one who hasn't found it yet?"

"Only because he wasn't looking."

"Your hacker was hacked."

"So was yours."

"Which means, whoever we're dealing with is slick. We have to be careful."

"Which is why I think we should call in to our respective offices and tell them where we are."

She whirled on him, planting her hands on her hips. "Call them when they both might be compromised? Are you suicidal?"

"No, but at the same time, if we don't call in, then we won't know what they're doing."

"Exactly, and it goes the other way, which keeps us alive."

"Or Mastermind hasn't been ready to kill us."

"We've only survived because we've been wily."

"I would have said lucky, and it's going to run out at some point," Darren said, rolling his shoulders, which caused a ripple effect on his chest. The blanket slid down, and her gaze got caught on admiring the delineated muscles of his pecs.

The sheet tented. Her eyebrow rose.

"We won't need luck if they can't find us," she said, taking a step toward him. His eyes caught the sway of her breasts and stayed locked. Because she felt ornery, she grabbed her shirt and slipped it on.

"What will we do in the meantime? Bounce around from hotel to hotel, fucking our brains out on as many continents as we can? Until when? When do we know it's safe?"

"Run?" Her lips pursed. "That sounds like a cowardly plan. I was thinking more of hunting down the members of our respective teams and questioning them until we discover the truth. Then we kill them."

"You're talking about murdering friends."

"Torturing, actually. We would only kill those responsible."

"What if they had a reason for their actions?" he asked. "Maybe a family member is being threatened."

"Their excuses aren't my problem. If they plot against me, then they are the enemy."

"So you'd kill even those you love?"

At that question, she bit her lip. "You are trying to question my morals again."

"Just attempting to figure out your line."

"I am the line. Cross me, and you're done." Said with all the confidence of a cold-blooded killer, yet when she had the chance, she'd spared him.

Would she do it again?

She didn't know, and it made her mentally itch, the way he carefully poked at her, questioning the life choices she'd made. She'd not had the same opportunities as he had. Easy for him to speak. He'd been raised with certain freedoms.

I wasn't.

She also wasn't about to debate her way of thinking. They had more important things to figure out than the supposed moral decay of her character. "We need a plan."

"I agree, but I'd like one that doesn't involve killing and torturing people right off the bat."

"It would be faster, but since you insist," she uttered with a deep sigh. "If we were to call them, and I mean *if*, what would we say? 'Hello, here I am, come kill me?'"

"We could try for a little more subtlety. Right now, they don't know we suspect them."

"Then they are stupid."

"No, not stupid, and quite possibly innocent. Even if there isn't a hack, I highly doubt there's more than one person involved in this. It's figuring out who that person is that's the problem."

"We need a way to flush them out. How long until this wedding you're planning?" The one he insisted on bringing her to as his plus one.

"Too long. Reaper isn't supposed to get hitched for a few more weeks."

"Move up the date."

At that, Darren grimaced. "All the plans have been made. Invites, reservations, everything."

"Why would anyone want such a big and fancy wedding?" Her nose wrinkled. "They should have eloped."

"Which negates the whole idea of throwing a big party to tempt any spies out of hiding."

"Given the current interest in harassing us, I don't think we need a big wedding to draw out the culprit. So long as we make a public appearance, I think someone will show."

"If we make ourselves bait too publicly, though, civilians will be harmed."

"So?"

"Again, can we keep the casualties to a minimum?"

A noise escaped her. "You and your delicate sensibilities. Fine. You and I will be bait. Somewhere not too public. Which means we will be sitting rabbits. Might as well shoot me now since you have no common sense when it comes to making plans."

The smile he gave her, sweet and intense, would have melted her panties if she wore any. "What if we had another wedding? A quick one. Right here. In this city. Call in a few of our friends who are in Europe."

"Are you suggesting we get married?" She immediately shook her head. "No. I am not ready for that kind of commitment."

"A fake wedding."

"Because you think whoever is spying on us is dumb enough to fall for a false priest? It won't work. It has to look real, or they'll know it's a trap."

"So we do it in a real church, with a real priest. The fact that we have a history together and have gone through some intense shit lately will make it believable."

"Except I don't want to be wed."

"It would only be temporary. We could get it annulled after."

Or not. She found herself torn on that matter.

"We have no idea if that will work. And it is extreme. Why not just rent a restaurant for dinner for two?"

"Because that looks like a trap. Think of it. A hitman wedding with a whole bunch of targets?" Darren gave her that smile again, the one that had her knees hitting the bed so she could crawl up his body and cover him.

"It is devious. Fraught with problems," she muttered, rubbing her cheek against his chest, loving the friction.

"Are you saying you can't handle it?"

She paused and eyed him. "Do you really think you can prick my pride into doing it?"

"Yes."

She nipped him. "You might be right."

"Switch that might with *always* and—hey."

The twist of his nipple had him arching, yelling and laughing at the same time.

"Your plan isn't completely without merit, but it is dangerous, could fail—"

"Or succeed, and you'll owe me an apology."

"I am assuming any oral apology will do?" She eyed him as she dragged the sheet down his body.

"So long as it's sincere."

"What if I make sure it's wet?" She grabbed hold of him. "And satisfying."

"Perhaps if you gave me a sample, I could let you know."

What am I doing? She was supposed to be making smart decisions. Not...oh to hell with it. Where Darren was concerned, she couldn't keep her head straight—or her clothes on.

She leaned up and stripped off her shirt, denuding herself before him, preening before his ardent gaze. She wiggled back a bit on the bed and then bent over, exaggerating the movement, sticking her ass in the air, bringing her face level with his groin. He already stood at attention.

She took her time, grabbing him, loving how his cock always pulsed when she first wrapped her fingers around it. A little *Hello, and thanks for touching me.*

A quick peek upwards showed him watching. He always liked to watch as she poked her tongue out and ran it over the tip of his cock.

"Lick me."

"Don't give me orders."

"Don't lick me."

"I'll do what I like," she said with a grin before she ran her tongue from the tip all the way down his shaft and back.

A heavy sigh rushed out of him, and his body trembled.

So, she did it again, a humming sound escaping her when the fingers on his left hand gripped her hair. He didn't guide her or do anything at all with his grip, just held her as she bobbed. Marina managed to swallow his cock, every inch, all the way. She sucked at his flesh, and it expanded. She hollowed her cheeks and pulled harder. He got even bigger. As she took him in and out, the flat edges of her teeth dragged along his tender skin. Back and forth, she gave him the moistness of her mouth while her hand fondled his sac, kneading his balls, feeling them pull tight.

He was close to the edge, and she increased her pace, hands flat on the bed so she could lean over him and bounce up and down on his cock, sucking while he trembled.

"Enough!" he finally gasped, yanking his shaft from her mouth. It let go with a loud, wet pop. She crawled up his body, and he grabbed her, pulling her roughly onto his chest so that he might kiss her passionately. He swirled his tongue into her mouth, and she moaned. He knew how she loved kissing.

She went to poise herself over him, but he surprised her. He flipped her off him onto her stomach. When she would have reared up, he placed a palm in the middle of her back to push her down while his arm wrapped around her thighs and pulled her ass up.

She couldn't help but gasp when his fingers slid between her thighs. He had no trouble stroking her, the slickness of her cleft wetting his digits, making it easy for him to rub. He used her own honey against her as he stroked her clit, teasing her nub until she couldn't help but rock against him, uttering soft cries.

"Now," she begged.

"Tell me you want me," he whispered, his body covering hers but his cock teasing by sliding along her cleft instead of inside it.

"I want you."

"Again," he said more harshly against her ear, the hot breath making her shiver as his dick continued its sensuous slide against her swollen flesh.

"I want you. Dammit. Fuck me."

He uttered a loud, growling groan and thrust his cock into her, sheathing it in one swift stroke.

She almost came, especially because he went deep, so deep he hit the spot. Her special spot.

"Again," she begged.

Out. In. Thrust. *Yes*. Her sex squeezed him as he worked himself in and out of her. His fingers dug into her thighs as he thrust.

Harder.

Deep.

Hard again.

Oh, yes.

She kept gasping and making noises as he slammed himself into her welcoming flesh. His fingers clutched her almost painfully as he came, thrusting one last time, pulsing inside her, drawing her own climax.

A scream erupted from her as she orgasmed, her channel fisting his cock, drawing every last ounce of pleasure that it could.

He collapsed atop her. Heavy, sweaty, and breathing hard.

She'd never been happier.

He, of course, had to ruin it. "I'm going to make some calls and see if I can find a place to have the ceremony tomorrow."

Ah, yes, the fake wedding. "So soon?"

"Why wait?"

Because she wanted more alone time with him. For once, she didn't want her time with him to be about a mission. Why couldn't it just be them, in a bed, making love like normal people?

She could almost hear Kristoff bark, "*You are not normal people. You are soldiers of the state.*" And soldiers never let pleasure come before duty.

CHAPTER EIGHTEEN

DARREN LOST COUNT OF HOW MANY TIMES THEY HAD sex that night. He knew it was only once the next morning, though, mostly because they had plans to make—and they were both getting a little chafed.

But, dammit, it was as if they both feared the future and wanted to cram as much pleasure in as they could.

Unlike the last time, they actually talked. Exchanged tidbits about their youths—hers sad compared to his. Yet she didn't seem to be bothered by the fact that most children didn't actually walk five miles to school in the snow and rain.

In between the serious moments, there was the more playful stuff, such as "I dropped the soap," and "Where's my croissant?" Which, he might add, he did go out and fetch.

As the time for their execution of the plan neared, the words became harder to find. There wasn't much to say while, at the same time, too much to be said, which made no sense.

Darren had come to realize that he cared too much for Marina. Despite her lies. Despite what and who she was. He'd fallen in love all over again, and this time, it was proving much more intense than before. He didn't just glow with the thought of her; he burned. However, she was right about one thing: they couldn't hide or run forever. They needed to do something to draw out their enemy. Or was it only *his* enemy?

The problem remained that they still knew too little. What was the purpose behind the attacks? And would his marriage to Marina provide enough incentive to draw the perpetrator out of hiding?

Did he really care? He was about to marry Marina. For real. She was right that a ploy to use a fake priest wouldn't pass a scrutiny test; therefore, he made arrangements as if this were an authentic ceremony.

Luckily, France didn't just have the best bakers of baguettes in the world, and the sweetest pastries, it had a goodly amount of churches. Some of them quite old and displaying the majestic splendor of days gone by.

Despite the urgency, his plan to do it that same evening didn't pan out. The best they could manage, which took some serious greasing of palms, was for the following day. Which was all right. It gave him time to book a church, find a suitable priest, bribe his way into getting a license—with their real names. He even arranged flowers and hired someone to play the organ. He also bought a tux.

With all the details squared away, it was time to

make the phone calls that would set their plan in motion.

He dialed Harry, who answered with, "Darren, this'd better be fucking you calling!"

"Were you worried?"

"Of course, I was fucking worried, you dick." The swearing a measure of how much, given Harry didn't curse all that often. "Where are you? What happened? You went silent after the hotel. Early reports claim a bomb went off. Hard to tell for sure with the fire."

"Been a lot of stuff burning lately."

"I heard about the school. You think it was arson?"

"I don't think. I know. And I'm getting mighty tired of being one step behind. Only one good thing has come out of this entire debacle." He paused before he dropped the bomb. "I'm getting married."

"Can you repeat that last bit? Because I could have sworn you said you were getting married."

"Because I am. Remember Francesca?"

"The girl who dumped you in Paris?"

Darren winced. "Yeah. Big misunderstanding."

"How do you misunderstand a girl packing her stuff and leaving?"

"She had her reasons." And he had his for lying to Harry. "Needless to say, we've reconnected and are now planning to tie the knot."

"Fuck off."

"I'm serious."

Harry stopped laughing. "You mean this isn't a joke?"

"Not in the least. Once we saw each other again, we

both knew." At least, he did. This was the woman who turned his world upside down.

"When's the happy event?"

"Tonight. In a little church in the south of France."

"What?"

"I was hoping you'd be my best man." Since he wasn't inviting his retired father anywhere near this mess.

"You'd better not be screwing with me."

"Would I lie to you?" Did skirting the total truth count?

"You're not giving me much time to wrangle a suit and a flight over."

"Sorry about that. We were impatient, and given we're already close to the city of love, we thought...why wait?" Darren glanced over at Marina, who was having her own conversation in Russian with Sergei. "So get your ass over here. Invite as many of the BBI staff as you'd like. On me, of course."

"Some might not be able to make it. I know Calvin won't want to leave Lily and Zoe alone after what happened." The incident being a crooked drug ring targeting Lily and her kid to get to Calvin.

"That's cool. See if you can get Mason, Ben, Declan, and Jerome, though." All single guys and former students of the academy. They also happened to work for Bad Boy Inc. The only team Darren trusted.

"What about Sherry?" Harry's wife.

"I know it might be tough to get a sitter for your kids on short notice." He wondered if Harry caught the hint that things might be more dangerous than expected.

"I can't believe the mighty bachelor is finally getting tied down."

Neither could he. A part of him knew the wedding, as real as it seemed, was a sham, yet he couldn't help a certain excitement. Even indulged in a bit of fantasy where he wondered if maybe, just maybe, they could hold off on the divorce part and give this thing a real go of it.

He realized Marina didn't love him. Hell, he wasn't sure how *he* felt other than confused. That didn't change the fact that being with her made everything seem brighter. He wasn't sure he wanted to let her go. She made him feel and want things, stuff like a home and a family, which was why, when he and Harry hung up, he asked, "What're your thoughts on kids?"

Marina's nose scrunched. "Sticky and loud."

"You don't like them?"

"I don't mind them, so long as they don't bother me or touch my guns. Why?" she asked.

"Ever think of having any?"

At the query, her mouth opened and shut. "Why are you asking?"

"Curiosity."

"It is more than curiosity. Do you want children?"

He shrugged. "Never really thought about it."

"Me either. But I guess I would. Have some that is. If I met the right person."

I'm the right person. The words sat on the tip of his tongue, but he held them in. He didn't want to tip his hand. Didn't want to admit that he'd stupidly fallen for her again. Not until he knew he could trust her. "Would you retire to have kids?"

"Me?" She blinked. "I don't know. Someone has to care for them, though, I guess."

"Harry and his wife have kids. Three of them, actually. She took a desk job after the first. And Harry followed, taking over a management position at BBI when they popped out the second."

She made a face. "That is definitely a point against them. I don't know if I could do the whole mom-at-home thing."

"It's not uncommon for the men to take on that role." Why did he argue it still? They weren't even married yet, nor was it a real damned wedding!

"Can we discuss this another time? We have more important things to plan. Now that we've used the phone here, we need to move. And keep moving until it's time for the wedding."

"Think they'll try and hit us before the ceremony?"

She shrugged. "Maybe. But after all the trouble we went through planning this, don't you think we should at least make an attempt to go through with it?"

He wasn't about to miss this wedding. And not because he hoped to flush out the mastermind behind all the plotting. Perhaps this would be the thing to tie Marina down so she didn't run away from him again.

She loaded up their stuff on the cart, hanging the suit he'd found and the dress she'd scored on it, both hidden by opaque plastic garment bags. When he tried to take a peek, she'd slapped his hand and declared, "Bad luck."

Given her superstition, it made him wonder if she'd found something old and blue to go with the new.

A glance around showed the room bare of their things. "Let's go," he said.

They exited the motel, gazes keen on everything around them. Wondering if at any moment someone would start shooting. They made it to the car they'd rented without being accosted, and the long car ride to the small town they'd chosen was event free—if he discounted the blowjob she gave him that almost saw them crashing.

The brief respite for lunch still had them arriving early, with hours to waste before the ceremony.

He would have enjoyed perhaps booking into another suite, making love to Marina again. Maybe twice. Then a leisurely shower.

She had other plans. They involved breaking and entering the building across from the church. They entered it from the back, going up two flights of steep stairs. He kept watch as she screwed with the lock, the click the sound of success that let them into the apartment.

A stale place with a Spartan appearance, the modern furniture with crisp lines and simple colors—grays, blacks, and whites, with beige walls—barren of personality. But where was its occupant?

"Whose place is this?" he hissed, keeping his voice down lest someone beyond the two doors he saw came rushing out with a gun or a knife.

"Antoine Gagnon. Currently out of town and not due back for three more days, according to his social media page."

So, no interruptions. He liked it, especially when a peek through the two doors showed an upgraded bathroom with a large walk-in shower and a bedroom that, while tight, did have a double-sized bed.

But it was the window Marina showed interest in. She peered out between the slats of the blinds, scanning the road before saying, "I'll be back. I need to grab some stuff from the car."

The stuff wasn't the wedding dress or anything like that. Nor a skintight catsuit to tease him. Pity, he had this fantasy where their wedding got interrupted; the bad guys came, as invited; and Marina, wanting to be part of the fight, ripped off a white princess gown to reveal curve-hugging latex.

She ignored him as she opened a gray case that didn't contain makeup or other girly accouterments, but rather a...

"Is that a scope?" he asked.

"No, it's a vibrator. Of course, it's a scope." She pulled it out and set it aside. Her next long case, with the name of a florist embossed on the side, opened to reveal a gun. A very nice one.

"Is that a sniper rifle? Where the fuck did you get that? I thought you went dress and shoe shopping." She'd taken a huge chunk of their funds to make those purchases.

"I made a few small detours."

"A sniper setup is more than a few small detours. Did you even get a dress?"

"Yes. You will be proud to know that it cost less than a hundred US dollars."

"And the rest of the money?"

"I used to buy stuff." She didn't elaborate as she set up the rifle with the scope, using a table to bring it level with the window ledge. She stretched out over the flat surface that was a few feet in length, her arm curved around the gun as she pressed her eye against the lens.

"Who are you planning to shoot?"

"Anyone who looks strange."

"You can't just fire off willy-nilly."

"It won't be erratic. I promise, each bullet will hit its desired destination."

The way she said it, so seriously, made him wonder if she might be a little psycho. Most definitely a killer.

She laughed as she peeked at him. "You should see your face. Do you really think I am so stupid as to start randomly killing people just because I don't like the looks of them?"

"At this point, I have no idea." Even scarier, he wasn't sure if he cared whether she was a killer. Look at her, humming happily as she aimed her scoped vision around the cathedral across from them. A pure pro.

"What should I be doing?" Since she obviously had no plans to do him.

"Make yourself look pretty for the wedding."

"Your attempts to emasculate me won't work. And besides..." He got close enough he could lean himself over her body, keeping only the thinnest of space between them, his lips close to her ear. "I don't need anything to look hot but you on top of me, naked."

Her breath caught. "We have to be careful from this point on. No more time for play."

"This isn't play," he said, running his hand over her shirt, tracing her upper back, lower, her waist, then the lean roundness of her hip. "This is necessity."

He needed one more time balls-deep in her, to imprint her on his skin. Remind her why they were so good together.

He kept his body over hers as he tugged at her pants. She'd chosen yoga style, the leggings pliant and easy to yank down. His zipper and button gave way next.

But he didn't immediately maul her. She pretended to ignore him, watching the street, and yet a swipe of his finger down her cleft came away soaking wet. He rubbed that moisture over her clit, and a shudder went through her.

He dipped into the tightness of her sex with a finger, loving how it gripped him. Loving, even more, the soft moan that slipped from her.

"Why can't I stop craving you?" he muttered as he sank behind her and licked at her honey.

She didn't reply, but neither did she move away. She rocked against his face as he lapped at her. Moaned as he stabbed her with his tongue. Cried out as he flicked her clit. When he thought her ready enough, he positioned himself on his knees behind her, the head of his cock, thick and blushing, eager for its own taste.

He pressed the tip against her wet slit. "Tell me you want me."

No hesitation. "I want you."

He sank into her, the pulsing heat of her around his cock, heaven. He buried his face in her hair as he thrust into her, feeling the slicked, wet pull of her pussy. She squeezed so tight.

He thrust, his hips pumping, and she cried out and clenched with each stroke.

It didn't take him long to get to the edge. His fingers found her nub and took her over first. He didn't let go until the spasm of her muscles milked his cock. He shot his cream. Came so fucking hard inside her, he almost passed out.

It was always that good. Always. He couldn't let her walk away. Not this time. Maybe not ever.

He nuzzled her hair, cradling her body, and said it. "I love you."

She didn't repeat it right away. He could have slapped himself.

CHAPTER NINETEEN

WHAT COULD A WOMAN SAY TO A MAN WHEN HE declared his love? How could she escape when he was still deep inside her?

It never even occurred to Marina to reply. Panic hit, and she only wanted to flee.

"I need to get ready. I'll grab the bags. You watch the church." She used their mission as an excuse to wiggle out from under him. Fled without even wiping herself, which meant cum oozed down her thigh.

Because he kept coming inside her. *And I let him.* Let him, even knowing her birth control capsule was gone. Her chip controlled more than her position on a map. She could be fertile at this very moment.

Even pregnant.

The realization had her slamming the bathroom door shut and leaning on it. What was wrong with her?

Nothing. She was perfect. Except for her crazy attraction to Darren.

It's more than attraction. She liked being with him. Liked him enough that she wanted to gasp, squirm—no, don't say it—cuddle.

Even more frightening, she wanted more than that. No.

Yes.

Why couldn't she admit that she loved him, too?

Because I can't. It wouldn't work. He was just a job. A means to an end. She had to distance her emotions.

How could she when he made his so obvious? Darren loved her. Loved Marina. Not Fran. He'd said it.

What had she done? She'd run away. Talk about an emasculating slap to his declaration. Also probably the best thing she could have done. Surely, her actions would make him change his mind. Which was a good thing. She didn't want him mooning over her. They were, after all, only working together.

We're getting married this evening.

Not a real wedding. She couldn't forget why she was doing this. Not for love, that was for certain.

She wanted to hide in the bathroom but couldn't. She quickly showered, and with dripping hair, made him lock the door behind while she jogged down to get their things from the car. When she returned, his eyes held a question, but she shook her head. "Clear so far."

"That's not what—"

Rather than talk, she fled and hid in the bathroom for as long as she dared. Applying her makeup, arranging her hair, eschewing her duties, and being a coward.

When she emerged, she wouldn't look him in the eye. She shouldn't see him. It was bad luck.

"I will dress in the bedroom." She didn't give him a choice, slamming the door behind her and leaning on it as if afraid he'd force his way in. He didn't. He probably regretted his words.

Surely, he didn't mean them. But why would he lie?

Get your head back on the mission. Time wasted while she acted like an emotionally crippled female. She got ready, sliding on the wedding gown, which wasn't traditional by any means. She couldn't bring herself to wear a pristine white dress to this sham. The one she'd chosen was elegant and practical. The blousy top hid the bullet-proof corset as well as the gun tucked under her arm. It tightened at her waist and then belled at her hips, with enough fabric to flare if she needed to make a sudden movement. The ornate sleeves could also be torn off in a pinch, giving her access to her knives. The shoes were practical flats, molding to her feet to give her the best ease of movement and grip.

She left her hair down, a moussed and wavy, controlled mess that framed her face. She kept her makeup simple, smoking her lids and darkening her lashes. A bit of lipstick to her mouth. When she was done, she looked elegant and wide-eyed. Surely, not frightened by a fake wedding?

The sound of the apartment door closing brought her out of the bedroom. No Darren in sight. She fled out the front door and saw his head already two stories down as he skipped the stairs fast.

"Come back," she yelled.

"It's bad luck. See you at the altar."

Dashing after him would look odd if anyone watched, but she could protect him from the window. She ran to it and pressed her eye to the scope, peeking through it and aiming lower to see the sidewalk and street.

Darren emerged from the building just as a taxi slid to a stop out front.

Her finger curled on the trigger then eased as Darren hugged the man who stepped out of the rear.

A gray-haired gent, and a warm embrace? Even without seeing the face, she guessed Harry.

They stepped into the church.

Out of sight, yet she didn't move. Couldn't.

The moment approached. The final one. Where she'd bind herself to this man for life. However short it might be.

Anxiety pulsed inside her. This entire idea was crazy. So crazy.

There was still time to stop it.

Except, next thing she knew, she was the one doing a lemming dash across the street, wondering if a sniper on a roof would use that moment to take her out. Or if a car would come screeching out of nowhere. Perhaps the earth would open up and swallow her before she set foot in such a holy place. She made it to the church doors unmolested, which meant she had to go inside. That required another deep breath, noisily expelled when she didn't burst into flames.

The interior of the church vestibule had a musty

smell. Age. God. Judgment. All in one place, weighing her sins. She had quite a few. Would the Christian God smite her for defiling this holy place?

She could hear organ music playing beyond the vestibule area. To the left and right more doors, two labeled with the universal signs of a man and a woman. Washrooms. The other said only *Office* in French. Another pair of doors beckoned straight ahead. They swung open, and she almost shot the man who peered out at her.

"You must be the bride." The man inclined his head. "Everyone's inside waiting." He thrust a bunch of flowers at her. "Darren said to give you this."

A bouquet of orchids. Her favorite flowers. He'd remembered.

She clutched them, wishing she could instead hold a knife or a gun. A weapon wouldn't make her hands shake like these flowers did.

The man, an American with dark skin and short, curly hair, held open the doors and waited for her to step through. Time to stop dithering. She entered and immediately paused as she saw Darren standing at the head of the church in front of an altar covered in white cloth, wearing a tuxedo that fit him perfectly. The man looked good. Damned good. Especially when he smiled at her. It made her stomach roll.

This is really going to happen.

There was no one to walk her down the aisle. She could have used a helping hand. But admitting to weakness was never an option. She held herself straight, tried to remember to breathe. She barely heard the music over the roaring in her ears just as she played scant attention to the audience, a failure on her part. She should have been taking note of faces and posture, yet she only had eyes for Darren.

He loves me. And he'd arranged this marriage because of it. This wasn't a plot for him. He wanted to do this.

Panic tried to claim her. It clawed, seeking a crack. Almost found one when the priest asked if anyone objected. What would happen if she raised her hand?

A ring, a cold band of metal he'd managed to acquire, slipped onto her finger like a vise that cut off circulation. She felt dizzy. Sick. She heard herself speaking words as if muffled underwater. "I do."

There was more talking after that, a blur of color and sound, then a kiss. A toe-tingling kiss that made it all the more horrifyingly real.

She opened her eyes and saw Darren watching her. It was done. *I'm his wife.* People clapped, a few even whistled. More than expected.

Turning to the crowd, she looked out upon the two-dozen or so that had managed to come. Friends of Darren's. Very few friends of hers. People fooled into attending a sham.

Does it have to be a sham?

He loved her. She loved him, too, even if she didn't want to. Fought it. Because she knew that love would die.

Today. In a few minutes. Along with a few people most likely.

I could stop it.

There didn't have to be blood spilled today.

There were papers to sign. As she wrote her name, her true name, in a big, sloppy scrawl on the document, a cake was wheeled in, a towering monstrosity with thick loops of icing and many plastic-looking flowers.

Darren entered his signature alongside hers.

It was done. They were married. She tucked the paper into her cleavage with a false smile. "Better keep that safe."

"A treasure for me to discover later," he murmured, wrapping his arm around her waist.

"Egads, look at those disgusting lovebirds," someone said.

Her stomach churned.

"I have to use the ladies' powder room." Marina fled before Darren could say anything. Averted her gaze from that cake and its sugary coating. Fled past all those people, even the ones she knew, who pulled out cigarette packs and planned a group smoke. She swept past the indicator for the washroom, pausing only before a door marked *Exit*.

She looked back in the direction of the church proper, where Darren stood waiting.

Waiting for me. Once again, he'd wait for a long time because she wasn't coming back. He was a job, and she'd just gotten it done. But could she really go through with the next step?

Sergei won't understand. Sergei also didn't have to live with the consequences.

With a sigh, she yanked the fire alarm, causing a siren to go off loudly. Only then did she exit the church.

A car waited, and she jumped into the passenger seat.

As Sergei sped off, he asked brusquely in Russian, "Did you sign the certificate?"

"I have it right here." She tugged it out of hiding and almost ripped it as the bomb went off behind them.

CHAPTER TWENTY

THE MOMENT THE ALARM WENT OFF—SCREAMING ITS strident warning—Darren knew they had little time. Their plan to draw out the enemy had worked. Something had happened, perhaps not inside the church, maybe not even yet, but it was only a matter of time before danger struck. And he'd lost Marina.

I have to find her.

It didn't matter that she could take care of herself. A man didn't let his new wife face danger alone.

Darren raced down the church aisle, ignoring the audience. Unlike a civilian wedding, these people didn't stupidly look around asking, "What's happening?" or screaming. They moved with quick and quiet efficiency, scattering in as many directions as there were exits. If this were a trap, they stood a better chance in small groups. He also saw more than one gun come out. He had to wonder how many of them suspected that this wedding was meant to act as bait and trap. How many operatives had Harry posted outside?

Darren trusted that those present could figure shit out and chose to go find his new bride. Every second he didn't see her reappear in her shimmering silver and black dress—which, while not traditional, did at least sport a billowy skirt—was a moment of miniature panic. Was she hurt? Dead?

He slammed into the woman's washroom and paid no mind to the possibility of anyone being in there. "Marina!" he yelled, not receiving a reply, and the room with its handful of stalls was not big enough to hide her. The window was too small for her to use as an escape.

Where is she?

Harry poked his head in. "Get out. Now."

He wanted to argue, but his friend's intense order had him striding then running, following Harry to the red *Exit* sign at the end of the hall. They shoved out into an alley between the old cathedral and the building beside it. A wide space large enough for a single car and not much else.

"We should—" Harry never did finish his sentence. An explosion sounded. The building shook, and stray bits of masonry fell from above, deadly missiles that had them both plastering themselves flat against the wall.

In moments, the rain of destruction ended, but the alarm kept ringing and ringing as a hint of smoke perfumed the air.

Darren pushed away from the wall. "Holy shit. That was close."

"Too close," Harry agreed with a grimace. "Thank goodness for that alarm."

"No kidding. A good thing you had your men do a sweep and found that bomb, or we'd be meat chunks right about now."

"Wasn't my guys. We were all in the church with you."

"Tell me you had rooftop snipers in place."

"Was I supposed to? Because you never said shit to me."

"Because I assumed—"

Harry held up a hand. "Hold on a second. Why would you think I'd have people sweeping the church and setting up stations outside?"

"Because this was a trap."

"You told me this was a real wedding."

"So that any moles listening would be fooled. Marina and I hatched this wedding to draw the person targeting us into the open."

"More like draw a bunch of us to one place and eliminate us in one shot. What the hell were you thinking? And why didn't you run this by me?" Harry clued in a second later. "Holy fuck, Darren, you didn't actually think I was a mole, did you?"

"Someone's been leaking our movements."

"And you assumed it was me or the gang at Bad Boy? They're like fucking family."

"I know."

"Then why..." Harry's expression hardened. "She made you think that."

"No." Yes. He shrugged. "We couldn't be sure, so we

set a trap. One that netted far more than expected. I need to find Marina and get out of here."

"She's gone," Harry stated.

"What do you mean gone? Did someone see her getting kidnapped?"

"Wake up and smell the fucking reality. She's gone because she's the one who tried to kill us."

Darren shook his head. "No, she wouldn't. We were working together."

"Were you? Or was she just stringing you along?"

"The person attacking me almost killed her, too."

"Or did she make it seem that way?" Harry headed to the mouth of the alley, the distant sound of sirens a sign they should leave or get caught up in a police and paperwork nightmare.

Darren kept pace. "Marina's been protecting me."

"Protecting you so well, you keep almost dying. Seems kind of hinky to me, or hadn't you noticed how all of her side of the church left only seconds after she excused herself?"

"You think Marina had a part in this?" Darren gestured to the church now sporting cracks in its century-old façade.

"I don't think, I know. Wake up, Darren. Look at the facts. This was no coincidence."

Much as Darren wanted to deny it, Harry appeared right. *She tried to kill me.*

No, not Marina. Sergei, he'd wager. That bastard must have done this, and she'd known of the plan and tried to save him by setting off the alarm.

"Where did she go?" he asked.

Harry shrugged as they moved away from the church and the crowd gathering. "No idea. I already told you we didn't have any eyes outside."

"How could you have no one watching?" Blaming Harry wasn't fair, and yet it was all he had.

"Because you didn't give me enough time. Or warning. It was all I could do to ensure you didn't get married alone."

Darren tugged at his tie and loosened his shirt. "The whole point of this wedding"—a sham of a ceremony because it turned out she'd played him all along—"was to draw out the enemy."

"You mean the one you were sleeping with?"

"Marina wouldn't kill me."

"The woman is a Russian operative."

A scowl twisted his face. "No need to remind me that I'm an idiot."

"Apparently, there is. I remember how wrecked you were the last time she left you."

"It was different last time. She was hired to spy on me."

"And this time, you hired her. But she was playing you all along."

"You don't know that for sure."

"I have a ruin of a church that says otherwise."

"I don't think she wants me dead." He did, however, believe she was caught up in a situation.

"At least you found out about her treacherous heart now rather than after a real marriage."

"Actually, it was real."

"Say what?" Harry swerved to look at him.

"It was real. We thought the whole wedding bait wouldn't work if we didn't get a real priest and stuff."

"Are you insane?" Harry shouted. "You married a Russian assassin."

The incredulity made Darren wince. "Yes, but in my defense, she's really hot." No blood to the brain when she was around.

Harry sighed. "Dammit. I'll have her taken care of."

"No." Darren shook his head. "I don't want her killed."

"After everything she's done? Why the heck not?"

"She pulled the fire alarm." Stated even if he didn't know for sure. "She warned me." It had to mean something.

"You are under this mistaken idea that she cares for you. I think it's pretty clear she doesn't. And I can prove it."

"How?"

"By putting you in the hospital." Harry took out his knife and came at Darren.

CHAPTER TWENTY-ONE

THE ECHO OF THE EXPLOSION RATTLED AROUND inside her head. It wasn't the first time she'd abetted a bombing. Yet this was the first time she worried about the repercussions.

More specifically, she worried about one person. Had Darren made it out in time?

Is he alive? Let him be okay. How could she know for sure?

She wanted to tell Sergei to turn around and go back so she could see for herself. She dug her nails into her palms, the sharp pain reminding her to bite back that request. Sergei wouldn't understand.

As it was, he grumbled that the job was botched. "I can't believe someone pulled the fire alarm. Probably teenagers. Always pulling pranks."

Sergei didn't believe in Occam's Razor. He failed to see the most obvious reason.

Which suited Marina just fine. "You were probably seen." When guilty, place the blame on someone else.

"I was most certainly not seen." The big man seemed rather insulted.

"Well, someone figured out something and tried to warn them." Sergei had yet to make the Marina connection. If he did, she'd lie, lie, lie. Only an idiot would admit her responsibility. Sergei had a bit of a temper.

Meanwhile, she still didn't know if she'd succeeded in rescuing Darren. If she did, then that meant she was still married, but for how long? Darren wouldn't hesitate to divorce, especially after her most recent actions.

Sergei tried to show optimism. "Maybe they didn't leave right away. The bomb might have caught a few. We will have to check the news and see how many died. We might be the number one story tonight, eh?"

Even she had to wince at the sacrilegious fact that they'd used a bomb in a church. In the damned cake, close to the altar! Not only had they blown up the Bible and any religious artifacts in the area, they might have gotten the priest, too. Would his death count as two sins?

"Even if the bomb didn't get anyone, it's not a big deal. Who cares if Darren lives? We got what we needed."

Brown eyes set under bushy brows perused Marina as Sergei took his gaze off the road. "The marriage might not be enough. Next time, I will go for something simpler, like a bullet to the head."

A sniper shot to end the only man to make her

regret the choices she'd made? She couldn't let that happen. "I don't want you killing him."

"Why not? I thought the whole point of the plan was to make you a widow." Because a widow without a prenup would inherit everything her husband had, including the academy of misfits he ran.

"He doesn't have to die for this to work. I'll just request the academy in the divorce."

"Which could take years." Sergei glared at her. She felt the heated laser of his stare even though she'd dropped her glance to the fine stitching holding the panels of black satin together. The right color for a funeral, not a wedding.

"What is a few more years at this point?"

"What is happening to you? We had a plan. Why are you diverting from it?"

She rolled a shoulder. "Things change." She'd changed. Sergei's brilliant plots no longer appealed. She'd gone into this for revenge. But now...how much more of her life would she allow it to consume? Should the sins of two people long dead taint anyone who ever came in contact with them?

"You are obviously on your period," Sergei grumbled. That was his answer to Marina whenever she did not behave as expected, which was why he didn't die. "Let me know when you are thinking clearly again."

That was the whole problem. She'd not had a single clear thought since meeting Darren. The media often joked about how men couldn't think around hot women because of a lack of blood to their brain. She'd say the same applied to women.

Darren confused her. The very fact that he affected her ability to reason was enough to kill. If he were dead, the problem would be solved.

Let Sergei shoot him. Wipe her hands clean.

I don't want him to die.

The song on the radio finished, and she heard a roaring white noise that muffled the host, but only after she'd heard the news. A male had been taken to the hospital with serious injuries after a church bombing. A man in a tuxedo.

It took forever to book into their hotel. Two rooms. Longer still for Sergei to settle down, finally snoring in front of the television in his room. Only then could she sneak out.

A taxi got her to the hospital quickly, because she had to see. See the man in the tuxedo and reassure herself that he lived.

She told no one she was going. Sergei, especially, wouldn't understand. He didn't have to know. In the morning, they'd board their flight to Russia and let lawyers begin the process of acquiring the academy. A piece in the puzzle of revenge.

So close to being done. At last.

She couldn't wait to pour a glass of vodka and celebrate their most recent win. She'd be home within the next day. Just one more night in a hotel. So why was she skulking out of her room and taking a taxi to the hospital? She hated them, the antiseptic smell a reminder—

Beep. Beep. All around things flash and scream. Machines with tubes and lights.

—of a little girl shuffled into a corner, eyes wide and watching.

The place is mostly white. White coats. White walls. White floors. All the better to see the red spray of arterial blood.

There is someone moaning. Her mother is on the rolling bed. And she is the source of the blood.

The little girl sucks her thumb. Watches with wide eyes. Still a bit deafened by the sharp crack of the fired bullet.

She would never forget the look of shock in her mother's eyes or her pleading to spare her child. *Spare my daughter. Please. Have mercy.* They showed none.

As the adults rushed to act, she was passed around, not speaking, in her own world as her clothing—covered in blood from both her parents—was stripped from her.

She'd lost her home that night, too. Everything from that point forward changed because of two men. Assassins who had orders to remove both of Marina's parents. They did so in front of a little girl eating her birthday cake.

Was it any wonder she had issues?

The assassins didn't shoot her. They'd left a witness to their callousness. Even laughed as they went out the door while blood pumped from her parents' bodies. Even at her young age, she'd known enough to dial for help.

Nothing could help. Even if the loss of blood hadn't killed them, the bullet wounds would have.

Marina could have forgiven a proper hit. Her parents, as she learned, had skirted certain rules and made enemies. What she couldn't forgive was the assassins giving a little girl nightmares. Because of them, she'd made a promise to her dying father that she would kill everyone who'd had a hand in his death.

But how far should it go?

She'd killed the original assassins. Then their team, which, two and a half decades later, had scattered around the globe. It actually worked in her favor. No one connected the dots.

However, their deaths didn't erase the nightmares. Who had funded the killers? Some rich drug lord and his partner. They died, as did their left and right-hand men.

It should have been enough, yet she still heard her father's raspy voice. "Avenge."

What was left? *Who'd trained them?* What about going after the school that thought it was okay to train men to kill people in front of little girls? What kind of depraved curriculum were they hoping to achieve?

What of the companies that provided them cover?

How far does it need to go, Papa? When could she say enough?

She'd spent every penny she made on her vendetta and would need more to go on. That turned out to be simpler than bringing down the businesses without repercussion. She'd erected crime rings in the cities she needed to hit. It gave her dollars, a base of operations, and an attack force that didn't link back to her. Although, it had gotten close recently.

She'd tangled with Bad Boy and only barely made it

out. Darren never knew. Never even guessed that she was the mastermind of so many plots.

But I wasn't behind the island. Someone else had gathered them all in that spot. And Sergei swore he had nothing to do with the helicopters.

Which meant there was another player. But would Darren suspect? Like everyone else, he'd blame everything on the Russians.

Whatever. It didn't matter.

Except it does because I don't want him to hate me. She just couldn't explain why that was important.

The hospital stood bathed in light, and she had the taxi drop her off a block away. She had no clear plan other than getting inside unseen. That was the easy part. More difficult was figuring out how to get into the hospital records to find the location of the victim of the church bombing—which the news reported as terrorism-related.

It took finding a quiet station, the nurse having grabbed her phone and a tampon before leaving it unguarded on the third floor. Marina quickly slid into the warm seat and grumbled at the log-in screen. Lucky for her, there was one thing that most workplaces had in common. Some people couldn't remember their passwords and...a peek under the desk didn't show it, nor was there a sticky note in sight, but she found something taped under the keyboard.

She tapped one of the hand-scrawled streams of letters and numbers. In moments, she had a direction to go.

The church bombing victim had scored a private

room on the fifth floor, but the file didn't say much else. Just a general description, no name, and the notes on his condition were blank, citing, "*see physician.*"

It might not be Darren. She still had to see.

The fifth floor at this time of day was quiet, the nurses' station at the far end of the hall and away from the door she wanted. A man leaned over the counter, chatting with the nurse.

The empty chair outside the door she sought probably belonged to him. The question remained, though, did anyone guard inside the room? If she were setting up the security, she would have someone.

Sneaking in wouldn't work. She'd need a distraction.

The man at the counter laughed at something the nurse said and leaned down to whisper something. Whatever it was had her standing, giving a quick glance around, then scooting off with him into another room.

How kind of them. Now, for whoever guarded the room. How to get them to exit?

Marina took a moment to test a few knobs before she acted, opting for the simplest ploy. She pounded on the portal then dove through the door of the room across from it, shutting it quickly, the wadded cotton batting shoved into the latch hole keeping it from latching. Flattening herself against the wall, she held her breath, listening.

It didn't take long to hear a masculine, "You see anything?"

"No, but Mason's gone. I'll check out in the hall. You stay with him."

Two men. One of them gone. She waited until the

steps receded before peeking. She saw the rear of a man at the end of the corridor, pausing at the nurses' station before turning the corner. She skipped across the way, whipping open the door and shutting it quickly as someone said, "Hands up."

Thank you for pinpointing your location. She turned and jabbed, the heel of her hand hitting the guy in the diaphragm. Then lacing her hands together, she swung them like a club at his head. He staggered. She raised her hands again, only to freeze at a voice.

"Hello, Marina. Looking for me?"

That sounded exactly like Darren behind her. Whereas, in front of her, lying in the bed, a still figure with the blanket drawn to the neck. Not Darren. Not even a real person. A bloody mannequin.

This is a setup!

She whirled, heart racing, and saw Darren, fully intact, still wearing parts of his tux, the white shirt, splattered with blood, gaping at the neck. His hair ruffled.

Then she got to see the angry mug of the man she'd taken down.

"You must be Ben," she said to the hairy fellow nursing a few bruises. "I've read all about you." Sergei had a few dossiers on the Bad Boy crew. He'd been known to headhunt for recruits.

"Please tell me I can kill her," Ben growled.

"No killing, not yet," Darren replied. "I need you to leave so Marina and I can have a chat."

"I'm not leaving you alone with her. She'll kill you."

"She didn't come here to kill me."

"Don't be so sure." Marina was beginning to realize just how rash and stupid she was, running over here to see him.

"Leave. Now," Darren barked when Ben would have argued.

"Don't expect a eulogy from me if she decides to send you over the rainbow bridge." Ben left, but she doubted he'd go far.

He'd already made his first mistake, though. He'd left her alone with Darren. Confusing things happened when they were together.

"You're alive," she said, brilliantly stating the obvious.

"I am, no thanks to you."

"You should thank me, considering you look remarkably whole."

"Don't you dare twist this around. Did you or did you not have a hand in the bomb going off today?"

Killers couldn't squirm when caught. She held firm. "It's business."

He advanced on her. "Is it business? Because I get the impression that I was supposed to die today. But someone saved me. Any idea who that was?"

Admit that she got cold feet? "I don't know, but Sergei wants to throttle them. You ruined his plan."

"His plan, or yours?"

More like her papa's ghost's. She shrugged as she backed away. "Does it matter?"

"I think it does. *Wife*."

A shiver went through her. "If you're not happy about it, we can divorce."

"Don't you mean annul? After all, we never consummated the marriage."

She blinked at him. In all her planning, that had never crossed her mind. In Sergei's plan, Darren died before the wedding night happened.

"You look a little shocked, *wife*."

"Stop calling me that."

"But that's what and who you are. My wife. Unless you're here to make yourself a widow." He lifted his hands away from his body, a defenseless target.

"I don't want you to die." The truth spilled from her, and she wanted to slap herself.

"Lucky me. Why did you want to marry me?"

"I need something you have."

"And you couldn't ask for it?" He arched a brow.

"Would you have given it?"

"I would have done more for you than you realize."

Would have. As predicted, she'd ruined his love. Again. "We don't have to let this end in tragedy. Just give me what I want, and we can go our separate ways."

"What about what you owe me?" he asked.

She blinked at him. "What are you talking about?"

"You lost, Marina. The bet. You said if Sergei were behind the leaks, you'd live with me for a month."

"But he wasn't. I was. For most of them, at any rate."

"Still your team at fault. Which means, I win the bet. And I'm demanding you fulfill your end of the bargain."

The moment what he said filtered in, elation filled her, along with incredulity. "You want me to live with you?"

"That was the deal. For a month."

She shook her head. "No. I can't do it."

"You have to. You lost."

"I never meant to agree to that."

"Then you shouldn't have promised." He reached out and snatched her arm. She could have hurt him to set herself free. Instead, she allowed him to reel her in. She was weak like that. For him at any rate.

"Why are you doing this?" she asked, tilting her head enough for their lips to align if he closed the gap.

"If you're looking for a concrete answer, I don't have one. I don't know why I can't let you go."

"Because you're weak."

"No, because, despite it all, I still love you." He drew her closer and walked her back until her ass hit the bed with its mannequin.

"You can't love me," she said.

"Shouldn't," he corrected as he fumbled with her pants.

"I wish you wouldn't," she muttered as she helped pull him free from his own trousers.

"You're like a drug I can't resist." His growled words as he pushed into her.

"You really should try. Because I have no use for you." A claim shown for a lie as she gripped him tightly and began to pant as he thrust.

"I keep thinking one last time. One last time, and I'll be cured."

"There is no cure." She'd tried. And now look at her. Legs wrapped around his waist, about to come all over his cock.

"Live with me for a month. Concede your loss, and maybe we'll finally sate ourselves."

Oh, the temptation. "It will never work."

"Don't." Thrust. "Be afraid." Out and then back in. His lips slid over hers as he murmured, "I only want to bring you pleasure."

But pleasure might make her forget her promise.

How much more blood must I spill for it? How much more happiness must she sacrifice?

She clutched at his head and kissed him as his pace quickened and he pummeled her willing flesh. Her orgasm after the tension of the evening hit her hard, yet she knew better than to scream. They weren't in a safe place. One wrong sound, and people might come running in. And then she'd have to kill them.

Instead, she buried her mouth against the meat of his upper shoulder, biting him when the climax rocked her body. They shook together in the aftermath.

He held her close. Kissed her temple. "Marina, I—"

Whatever he might have said next was lost in a hail of gunfire in the hall.

CHAPTER TWENTY-TWO

NOTHING WORSE THAN GETTING CAUGHT WITH YOUR dick creamed and still pulsing when a gun battle breaks out.

He quickly stuffed himself back into his pants, whereas she just yanked her pants up and then palmed a gun before hitting the door.

He heard someone yell, a cry of pain from close by.

Ben!

With no regard for the danger in the hall, Marina opened the damned door, poked her head out, and fired. *Pop. Pop.* She ducked and yelled, "Get ready to grab his arms and yank when I stand up."

She heaved in a deep breath and opened the door again when the latest barrage slowed.

Pop. Pop. "Argh."

Darren only vaguely heard the noise as he heaved Ben, dragging him inside. The man was bleeding from the shoulder and leg. Marina leaned back in, not an ounce of fear on her face. Excitement made her eyes glitter. "Two gunmen, one at each end of the hall. The one by the elevator is injured."

Not to mention brazen. Who the fuck sent a hit squad to a hospital?

"Is this your doing?" he snapped as he grabbed the sheet on the dummy and used it to press against Ben's shoulder wound.

"Don't insult me." She wrinkled her nose. "This is sloppy."

"Sloppy can still kill, and this will draw the cops."

"True, which is why I am going to clear a path for you and your friend."

"You can't go out there by yourself. You said there were two gunmen."

"Not for long." She poked her head out, ducked when someone started shooting, and fired from floor level.

The gunfire stopped.

"Only one left by the emergency exit," she announced.

She threw herself into the hall, and he yelled, "Marina." Then more softly, "Marina," as the gunfire erupted again, interspersed with a steady *pop, pop*.

Self-preservation said to stay in the room. His damned heart made him open the door.

He was in time to see her last shot take down the gunman. He crumpled to the floor, and Marina whirled, gun still raised.

Eyes flashing.

Body vibrating.

Lips parting.

Yelling, "Get down."

Darren obeyed and hit the floor, rolling as he did, hearing the dual gunshots fired. He ended up on his stomach facing away from Marina and thus saw a third gunman still standing within the open elevator drop, a perfect dime-sized hole in his head.

"Nice shot," he remarked.

But Marina didn't reply.

He whirled to see her down the hall, entering the stairwell, clutching her arm. Her bleeding fucking arm because she'd taken a bullet meant for him. Saved his fucking life.

He took a step after her as voices yelled, "Roll call." The academy boys who'd come to lay the trap converged, calling out their names. Only Ben and Marina were seriously wounded, but she'd disappeared. Darren wanted to go after her. However, chaos locked down the hospital. The cops wouldn't be happy until they'd questioned everyone. Darren had to return to his bed and play up his injury. The wound Harry had given him to have it look good in pictures. The mannequin got tossed down a laundry chute. And the dead bodies of the thugs were rounded up and declared a gang.

Darren was released the next day, but Marina's trail was cold. It was as if she'd vanished, again, leaving him more confused than ever.

The trap at the hospital proved only one thing. He knew nothing.

She'd come to the hospital to find him. Not kill him. She'd made love to him because of their connection.

Not to kill him. She took that bullet to save him. Not kill him.

What did it all mean?

Fingers snapped in front of his eyes. "Darren. Wake up. We're about to board the flight back home." Ah, yes, the airport Harry had brought him to after the hospital fiasco. Authorities were more than happy to see the tourists leave after their run-in with local violence.

Except, Darren wasn't ready for home. "I'm not going with you."

"What are you talking about? Of course, you are."

"I still have business here."

"This'd better not be about that Russian woman again."

"That Russian woman is my wife."

"Only until the annulment goes through. I've got a lawyer working on a judge for that."

Time to stop that plan in its tracks. "You can't annul it. We consummated the marriage."

"When? You were never alone after the ceremony."

"We had time at the hospital."

"For like two minutes!"

"It was long enough."

Harry cursed. "Goddammit. You were supposed to question her, not give it to her."

"I got some answers." And more questions. *Why did she take that bullet for me?*

Only one person could answer that, which was why he ditched Harry at the airport, despite all protests, and called his new friend in the city. "Pierrot. It's me, Fran's ex-boyfriend. Still want to make some money? I need you to get me to Russia without anyone knowing."

He needed to pay a visit to Marina. Because not only did he want to know why but he also intended to make sure she didn't welch on their bet.

CHAPTER TWENTY-THREE

THE VODKA BURNED ALONG THE GASH IN MARINA'S arm. A souvenir from her visit to the hospital. The furrow the bullet left hadn't hit anything major but required her to slap on several plastic adhesive strips and change shirts before hitting the airport. Airport security agents would make a fuss about blood on her shirt when what they should really be looking for was the knife concealed in her carry-on. The garrote around her wrist was hidden in plain sight as a bracelet.

The whole plane ride home—which involved several flights switching back and forth to lose anyone trying to follow—she couldn't decide what was more annoying. Was it the fact that she couldn't dress her wound properly? Or listening to Sergei berate her for not only sneaking out—as if she were a child in need of a chaperone—but also raging about the fact that she'd gotten injured because she defended a man?

He's not just any man. He's my husband.

The ride from the airport to her apartment—with Sergei accompanying her, probably to make sure she didn't turn around and board another plane back to Paris—was spent listening to him gibber at his wife on the phone and telling her he'd be home soon. But even that was delayed as he made a few stops. One to the liquor store. Then to the restaurant where he insisted on getting them dinner and then spent the meal enumerating the ways she'd failed him.

Once in her apartment, he complained again when she peeled off her coat, shirt, and then the bandages. "You just had to get injured. This will cut into upcoming projects."

"You got me a modeling gig?"

"With Pierrot. Apparently, you impressed him with your skills."

"Pierrot is a moron. I won't work for him."

"What if I got him to double your regular fee?"

"Make it triple, and I'll think about it." She held her arm over the sink and took a swig of the alcohol before sluicing the wound again.

Sergei slammed a cupboard shut and slapped a metal tin on the counter. "Give me your arm. You'll need stitches." Sergei might simmer and rail against her actions, but he still wielded the needle and thread deftly to close her gash.

"Ow," she complained as he began to stitch.

"Don't be a baby."

"Says the man who's usually a lot drunker before he lets his wife sew him up." She took a few pulls of the vodka, letting the burning heat ease the pain.

"Don't complain. It is the price you pay for your stupidity."

She didn't bother arguing. Sergei wouldn't understand. Her heart just wouldn't listen to her. Sergei called her weak and stupid. He was probably right. She and Darren were an impossible fit. Yet when she saw him in danger, she could only think of saving him.

Sergei snipped the thread. "Don't sleep on it, and keep your sleeves short. And remember to rub that lotion Kristoff gave you on it."

"Yes. Yes. I know how to take care of myself."

"Are you sure? Because I've seen no sign of it recently."

"I'm fine."

He harrumphed as he put the supplies away. "I will have Ivanka fill the fridge for you."

"She doesn't have to. I'm not an invalid. I can shop. It only grazed me," she remarked, wagging her arm.

"It shouldn't have touched you at all."

"You're not going to start that all over again, are you?" She rolled her eyes. "I took off and went to check on Darren. Forget about it already. Since when are you the overprotective uncle?" Yes, uncle. But in the field, they made sure to keep it professional.

"I still don't understand why you went. I told you I'd find out if that was your husband in the hospital."

How to explain that she needed to see him herself? "Yeah, well, you'll have to get over the fact that he's still alive." And he'd set a trap for her.

"For now. We'll see how long that lasts."

"I told you, I don't want him killed."

"You might not have a choice. We've been intercepting some of his staff's communications. The fellow running the agency has been making calls to have your marriage annulled."

"He can't. We consummated." Darren had seduced her, which still puzzled her. Why did he want to remain tied to her?

"So that's why you went to the hospital." Sergei grinned and clapped her on the back. "Good girl. Why didn't you say so? Although, I still say we should kill him. Much faster than a divorce."

"No. No killing. He has nothing to do with my parents' deaths."

"His father was running the school when those scum trained." Sergei scowled. He still hadn't forgiven the murder of his sister.

Uncle never let Marina forget, either. It was what he'd trained her for from a young age.

"Once we have the academy, then what?" Would the vendetta finally end?

"We blow it up."

"We could blow it up now."

"And he would just rebuild. If we own it, then it won't rise from the ashes."

She couldn't help but roll her eyes. "This is dumb. It's just a school." A school for second chances. A place for misfits who didn't belong anywhere else in the world. Marina understood the feeling.

"Don't forget what I've taught you. The enemy must be destroyed. You promised your father."

Guilt speech delivered, Sergei left, slamming the

door of her apartment. She chugged more of the vodka and slouched in a chair, the long neck of the bottle dangling from her fingers. The sun had set, and she had a gorgeous view of the city, the lights of it glistening like jewels.

I had to accomplish so much to get here. But had her life turned out differently, she might not have had to struggle at all.

She sighed.

"Why so glum? Did your handler ream you out for failing your mission?"

Hearing his voice here, in this place she considered sacred and secret, surprised her, but she didn't let it show as he emerged from her bedroom. How lax to not have searched her place first.

"You shouldn't be here." She took a sip from the bottle and hoped he didn't hear the trembling in her voice.

"We have unfinished business, wife."

"Are you here to serve me divorce papers?"

"Why would I do that after all the trouble you went through to marry me?" He circled around to the front of her chair.

"Marriage was a means to an end." She'd come up with the plan after she realized she couldn't outright kill Darren. She'd convinced Sergei it was a better idea.

"How did you know we'd marry? I hated you a few days ago."

"My aunt has a saying about love and hate." She'd gambled on his love overcoming that hate.

"You didn't do this out of love. Was it money, then?" he murmured aloud.

She snorted. "I have no need of your money."

"Then what possible motive could you have to want to be my wife? To spy? A girlfriend would have just as much access to me. So why the extra step?"

"A wife inherits her husband's things. The original plan called for me becoming a widow." And either he was playing dumb, or he'd not understood her Russian conversation with Sergei about the plot.

"You were going to kill me for money?"

Instead of replying, she asked another question. "How did you find me?"

"You might tell me that BBI and my students suck at their jobs, but not because I don't have the best teachers money can buy. Peter, my professor of technology, did some digging for me."

"And what did he find?" she asked, faking a casualness she didn't feel as she took another gulp of the vodka.

"Lots of Russian connections. Funny how everything we've been dealing with has led back to one place."

"Blame the Russians." She rolled her eyes. "How original."

"Don't pretend. You know who the mastermind is."

Only some of the time. "And if I do?"

"What does Sergei have on you? You're obviously working for him. Whatever it is, I can help. I can get you away from him."

The earnest plea would have seemed grand unless

one knew the truth. "I see your man isn't as good as you think."

"What's that supposed to mean?"

"Sergei and I are working together. As partners."

That caused him a moment's pause. "But you said he was your handler."

"I said many things. Some of them not entirely true. Sergei is my handler, but we decide things together." Which took quite some arguing. He liked being in charge.

"You were in cahoots with him the entire time." He said it with such incredulity, broken with sadness. "I have been such a fucking moron."

"Not entirely your fault. You didn't know I was lying." Or why. "For example, my parents didn't give me up. I was orphaned. Ask me how they died."

"How did they die?"

She fixed him with a stare. "They were celebrating my birthday with me at home when their killers broke in. They shot my parents in front of me. I was five."

His mouth rounded in horror. "Holy fuck, Marina. I'm so sorry."

"Sorry doesn't bring them back."

"Why do I get the impression you're telling me this has something to do with the marriage thing?"

Now, for the truth. The thing she couldn't escape no matter how good the sex was. "Because you're part of my revenge."

"Me? I wasn't the one who shot them."

"I know. I killed those responsible. I wanted vengeance. But it was over too fast, so I set out to find out who trained them. Who sent them on that mission. I'm almost done killing those responsible."

"You're talking about something that happened close to thirty years ago."

"It took me time." She shrugged. "I'm patient."

"If you know I had nothing to do with it, then what was the point of getting close to me?"

"The academy. I wanted to know for sure if Secundus trained my parents' killers. Once I knew it had, I set out to acquire it."

"By marrying me?"

She nodded, seeing the light in his eyes dying. The regard he'd held for her hardening. She understood in that moment that, until then, he'd harbored hope that she had done everything for love.

Truthfully? Some of it, she had. But he'd never believe that now.

"Let's say you get the academy and knock it off your revenge list, then what?" he snapped at her, his query hot and angry. "Kill all the teachers? The students?"

She shrugged. "I don't know. I imagine, one day, the need for revenge will fade." One day, the ghost of her papa would stop asking her to avenge.

"Violence is a vicious circle to break."

"How do I stop when it's all I've ever known?" She truly wondered. If she didn't have it consuming her, what would she fill that space with?

"You'd better figure it out, and quick, because I can't give you the academy."

"You have to." Or else everything she'd done, all she would suffer, would be for naught.

"And if I don't? Then what? You'll kill me? Go ahead. You've already taken my love and self-respect. Might as well get the whole fucking shebang." He bared his throat.

She couldn't move.

He snapped, "I said kill me, goddammit. You said being a widow was what your plan entailed, right? The bomb in the church then the attack in the hospital. All plots to kill me after the ceremony."

"I had nothing to do with the hospital."

"But you knew about the church."

She didn't lie. "I tried to save you."

"I know, which is why you're still alive. Why didn't you do it?"

"I don't know."

"Why did you save me in the hospital?"

"I don't know."

"I think you do." He advanced on her, eyes blazing. "Why won't you say it?"

Her mouth opened and shut, the words he wanted caught in her throat. Once spoken, she'd have to change her purpose in life because she couldn't have Darren and her vengeance, too.

"Say something, dammit." He grabbed her by the arms and shook her. "Why didn't you kill me?"

He kissed her, and she couldn't push him away. She could never do that.

He exploited her weakness, her love for him. Passion ignited, and they couldn't stop themselves. Their clothes were shed until flesh pressed against flesh. The sex happened quickly.

Frantic. Slick skin. Pounding hearts. Harsh breaths. The climax sudden. Intense.

He leaned his forehead against hers. "Say it."

"I—" Despite it all, the words remained stuck. How could she choose him over her parents? "I can't." She shook her head. "You need to go."

"Dammit, Marina. If I go, that's it. I'm not coming back." His gaze blazed, and she melted in it, opened her mouth, and the face of her father rose. *"Avenge me."*

She closed her eyes and dropped her gaze.

He sighed and pushed away from her. She heard the rustle of clothes being straightened. The door to her apartment slammed shut, and she winced. He'd left. Left her alone. Sad. Tired.

How much more, Papa?

For a moment, she saw his visage, and she waited for the demand his ghost always made, only to have it superimposed by that of her mama's, her gaze soft and loving. From her, a whisper. *"Live."*

The time had come to let the dead rest. Time for her to embrace a future.

With Darren. She had to catch him before it was too late.

Marina ran to the door, only to have it open on Sergei.

"I knew you were weak!" Sergei announced, his brows beetled into a thick, hairy line.

She backed away. "It's not what you think. I was coming to tell you he was in town."

"Liar. You care for him!"

"I don't. I swear, Uncle."

"Then you will let me kill him."

"No!"

"Then you leave me no choice." The knowing smile on his lips wasn't what brought the chill to her body. That occurred when Sergei raised the pistol and fired.

"You treacherous—"

Thump. She hit the floor too fast to properly curse him out.

CHAPTER TWENTY-FOUR

ANGER MADE DARREN LEAVE. HE'D GONE TO RUSSIA, taking a red-eye flight and then bribing his way into Marina's building to confront her. To find out why she'd saved him. Only to discover more lies. Nothing about Fran or Marina was real.

Except that you're good together. But was it enough? He'd wanted to find out, but she just couldn't commit. Wouldn't admit they had more than good sex in common.

And even if she did tell him she loved him, could he believe it? She'd lied about everything else.

He'd made a mistake coming here. Made a mistake thinking the things she'd done meant something. He'd leave in the morning and do his best to forget her.

The hotel he'd chosen had only the barest necessities, definitely no room service, which was why the brisk knock at his door had him frowning. No one but a select few knew he was here. He'd not even told Marina.

A woman of her skills, though, could hunt him down. Had she changed her mind? He had to wonder when a peek through the hole showed a burly man pacing.

"Who are you?"

"Sergei."

Could be a coincidence. He eyed the man with a stocky build and short-cropped, brown hair liberally streaked with gray. "Sergei who?"

"Just Sergei. And you know who."

"What do you want?"

"We need to speak."

"I highly doubt that."

"It's about Marina."

"What about her?"

"I am not shouting her business in the hall. Let me in."

A coward would have called security. Darren palmed his gun before opening the door.

The large Russian stalked past muttering, "Where is she? What have you done to her?"

"If you're talking about Marina, then I didn't do shit. She, on the other hand, has been busy yanking my chain."

Sergei whirled on him, eyes blazing. "Which is why you are angry with her. Perhaps you have killed her."

"I didn't kill Marina. Last I saw her, she was sipping vodka and explaining how this entire past week was a plot for her to marry me." Then she was creaming his cock and still refusing to say she loved him.

"She was alive when you last saw her?"

"Yes. Why?"

"She is missing." With that blunt announcement, Sergei spun around and began stalking back to the door.

"Wait a second. What do you mean missing?" Darren asked, but Sergei kept going.

Don't care. Don't care. Darren jogged to catch up to the man by the elevators. "Where is Marina?"

"Not here with you," Sergei said in a heavy accent. He stepped into the open cab, and Darren had a choice.

He jumped in with him. "Why did you think she was here with me?"

"Because she is not at home. When she is not at home, she is at work." The piercing eyes pinned him. "And you are work."

"Not anymore. I'm done with her."

"Humph. And this is why you make a poor husband."

"I would have made a great husband if this was a real marriage," Darren argued.

"Doubtful."

"How about you worry less about my husbandly qualities and more about the fact that Marina is missing. I'm going to guess you tried calling her cell and triangulating her signal."

A dark look answered that question.

"Do you suspect foul play?" Which wouldn't surprise Darren, given who and what she was.

"The cameras at her place—"

"You have cameras there? Why are you spying on her?"

"To keep her safe. The video shows nothing after you leave."

"They stopped recording?" Darren asked.

"No, they recorded, but a review showed no one entering or leaving the apartment."

"The door isn't the only way out," Darren observed. "What about through a window? She's only one floor from the roof."

"The windows are sealed, and Marina would never climb out through them. She doesn't like heights."

"Bullshit. I saw her jump out of a plane."

"She doesn't let her fear control her. Unlike some." Spoken with a sneer at Darren.

Exactly what was the big Russian implying?

The elevator dinged, and the metal cage slid open. Sergei immediately began walking. Darren kept pace.

"I highly doubt the front door to her place is her only escape route." Smart mercenaries always had a backup.

"Let's say she does have another way out and she used it. Why is she not contacting me?" Sergei wagged his phone.

"Perhaps she's upset and doesn't want to talk."

Sergei stopped dead. "If she is upset, then that would be your fault. She was perfectly fine until you came along and ruined her."

"I ruined her? She's the one who played me for a fool."

"Yet you are the man who makes her forget her mission. Who has her foiling a perfectly good bomb plot, refusing to kill you?"

"Maybe she's refusing to kill an innocent man because she has morals."

"She wasn't raised to show weakness."

"Sounds like you're part of the reason she's so closed off."

The eyes, under bushy brows, glared. "I trained her. She was a perfect soldier until you broke her."

"I broke her?" Darren couldn't help his incredulity. "Listen here, jackass, I'm not the one who stole a vulnerable little girl and stuck her in some special school you Russians have to indoctrinate kids. She was a child, not a soldier." He made a bit of a leap stating this, assuming some of what she had told bordered on the truth.

Sergei laughed. "She told you she went to a special school? That's funny."

A sigh escaped Darren. "Let me guess. That was a lie, too."

"Not entirely. It was special. But the school was my house. She lived with my wife, my brother, Kristoff, and our children. We were her teachers."

"Congratulations, you raised a psychopath."

"A very fine one, too, until you. Which is why you're going to help me fix her."

"Fix her how?" Darren asked. He and the big Russian had ended up outside, standing by a car.

Sergei didn't answer. Rather he popped open the trunk of a large navy-blue sedan. He rummaged around inside before emerging with an aerosol can.

Before Darren could ask him what it was for, Sergei sprayed him and he—ZZZZZZ...

CHAPTER TWENTY-FIVE

THE TRANQUILIZER DART WORE OFF, AND MARINA woke but pretended she still slept as the last of the drug eased from her system. She spent that time listening for clues.

She heard nothing but the drip from a faucet. Was she alone?

Upon opening her eyes, she let out a blustery sigh, mostly because Marina recognized the room. She'd spent much of her youth here, training with her uncle and cousins. Exercising daily for hours, despite bruises and aching muscles.

The cement block walls had been painted recently, a fresh change from peeling gray paint. The black foam mats underneath, however, looked worn. Along the edges of the walls was more equipment. Rope, thick and thin, all kinds, depending on the training exercise. Another wall held a rack with weapons, stubby knives to four-foot-long swords. Only the guns were kept locked up.

She noted a black bar bolted in front of an equally shiny mirror. Did they now teach ballet?

As familiar as the room was, the chain she was strung from, upside down, was new, the tub full of broken glass under her not promising, and the fact that she didn't dangle alone disturbing.

What have you done, Sergei?

Dangling across from her? Darren, his eyes closed as if he slept.

He probably did. Last she recalled, her uncle had darted her. Apparently, he'd done the same to Darren. But why?

"Darren. Are you awake?" she asked.

"Really hoping I am imagining the fact that I'm hanging eight feet off the ground over a tub of pointy shit."

"No dream. This must be one of Sergei's new traps."

"How do we escape it?"

Knowing her uncle? "One of us has to die."

"Excuse me?"

"This is a game where only one player walks away." It took only a moment for her to guess how it worked. She pointed. "There is a platform on either side. If you swing your body, you can grab hold and pull yourself up."

"What's the catch?"

"I'm guessing the person on the other end of the chain will get dropped.

"Pincushion city. Ouch. There must be another way."

"Doubtful. Sergei is pretty thorough. If he wants only one of us to walk away, then only one of us can walk away."

"Why would he do this? I thought he was your trusted handler," Darren mocked angrily.

"He is punishing me because of you. He says you make me weak."

"Do I?"

Yes. "No. But he thinks I am because we had sex."

"Seriously?" He waved a hand around. "Even you have to admit this is a pretty elaborate setup because he's mad you dropped your panties for me."

"Not elaborate for Sergei. My uncle—"

"Uncle! What the fuck? How come you're just now telling me he's related to you?"

"You never asked."

He mumbled a few choice curse words under his breath. "Well, that explains a lot. I defiled his niece. If he hates me so much, then why doesn't he just kill me?"

"Because then I won't learn my lesson. He wants me to kill you." To make a conscious choice to choose herself over Darren.

"Why is it important for you to do it?" he asked, poking at her. Constantly trying to get her to admit the problem, which was...

"Because you make me forget who I am."

"Is that a bad thing?"

The correct answer was *yes*. She settled for, "I don't know."

He stared at her.

She fidgeted and sighed. "Caring for you isn't bad, but it is complicated. I promised my father revenge."

"Judging by what you told me, I'd say you got it."

She had. But, apparently, Sergei didn't agree. "My uncle is counting on me. My mother was his sister."

"And, again, you did more than your part in avenging her. Isn't it time to let go?"

"You're just saying that because you want to live."

"Yeah, because not wanting to die is so selfish. But did it ever occur to you that what I really want is for you to be happy? Stupid me, I'd hoped you could find that with me."

"I did." He was the one person capable of pushing away her nightmares.

"I just wasn't enough. I hope you find what you're looking for in life, Marina." He closed his eyes and crossed his arms.

She blinked at him. "What are you doing?"

"Nothing. I must be the world's dumbest bastard, but I want you to live. So, take the escape."

"But I don't want you to die."

"You said we both couldn't live."

"I did. However, it is I who should die. You're a better person than I am. You escape." She crossed her arms.

"Careful, Marina. That almost sounded like you cared."

"What if I do care?" She finally admitted it. And the ghost of her father didn't arrive to smite her.

"What happened to 'it's just business'?"

"Don't use my words against me."

"Why not? I have nothing else to use."

"This is all your fault." She'd never questioned her purpose until she met him.

"How? Because from where I'm dangling, this is your fault. You came barreling into my life. You turned it upside down."

"Don't blame me. Because of you, I'm weak."

"It's called being in love."

"Which is weakness. You are both weak," Sergei exclaimed, stomping into the room. "What is wrong with you, Marina? I put you in here so you could kill him."

"I won't." She glared at her uncle. "I've done enough killing."

"What of your revenge?" he blustered.

"Don't you mean your revenge? Keeping our niece focused on a vendetta won't bring your sister back." A new player entered the room, her steely-eyed Aunt Beth. "Enough is enough, Sergei."

"It is enough when I say it is."

Aunt Beth glared and tapped her toe.

"Perhaps we are almost—" Her aunt cleared her throat. "Ahem. I mean, we are done. Or we will be once Marina smartens up." He tossed her a glare as if it were her fault that Aunt Beth harangued him.

"What exactly are you doing with Marina? I thought we agreed no more using the children as test subjects with your traps."

"She thinks she is in love with this weak American. I am making her strong again."

"What is wrong with her loving him? I'm American. Does that mean you don't love me?" Living in Russia for as long as she had meant Aunt Beth wouldn't back down from Sergei.

"Our love is different."

"How?"

"Because it is. Completely different situation."

"Really? Because, as I recall, you got me pregnant and kidnapped me until I agreed to marry your worthless ass."

"You were playing hard to get. I knew you loved me."

"Ha."

"Admit it, woman." Sergei lapsed into Russian, to which Beth replied rapid-fire.

Beth eventually switched back to English. "I'll admit I love you, but only if you stop with this revenge thing. Enough is enough. Leave Marina alone. You know that's what your sister would have wanted. And if Marina wants this man, then let her have him. She's tried hard enough to keep him. Look at how she fought to keep him alive during the helicopter incident."

"What do you know of that?" Marina asked.

Aunt Beth's cold smile had all the warmth of a wolf in the midst of a lean winter. "You chose to save him instead of just yourself. Just like you couldn't kill him in Paris, or the hospital, or even before all that on the island. Which, by the way, took care of two players bidding for an upcoming job and that annoying prat, Stefanov."

"You were behind those attacks?" Marina couldn't have said who was more surprised, her or Sergei.

"Yes, it was me. Don't think I didn't notice how you tried to bury Marina in work to get her to forget that man. Anyone could see she moped for him." Aunt Beth cast Darren a sly look. "But, she was too stupid, like her uncle, to act. So I nudged her, via my island plot. I maneuvered some players into one spot, then threw Marina at him so she could decide what she wanted. When she still couldn't decide, I threw danger their way. I'd say judging by her actions, she's made her choice."

"You are more devious than I am, wife."

"I know. It's why you love me. Now, come. If you must glare at something, then glare at Natasha's new beau."

"What beau? She is not allowed to date. She is only twenty-four."

Sergei went ranting out of the room, and Aunt Beth winked at Marina. "Be sure to stay in touch." She slapped a button and left.

The pulleys holding up Marina and Darren jerked and moved over a few feet before they lowered with a mechanical whine and rattle until they were safe on the floor. Brains still in their uncracked heads, bodies not sporting any holes they shouldn't.

They made quick work of the restraints binding their ankles, her faster than him. The moment he was done, she threw herself atop him.

"Oomph." He gusted out a breath before wrapping

his arms around her. "Does this mean you're happy to see me?"

"Yes."

"Is that wise? Your aunt just admitted to being the mastermind who almost killed us."

"I should have known. She always was our most thorough teacher." Her lessons could make a student bleed.

"Your family is nuts."

Certifiably. "I don't want to talk about my family." She wanted to devour his mouth. Imprint herself on him. She sucked at his lower lip. Nibbled on his tongue.

"Someone." In between nips. "Might be." Soft moan. "Watching."

"If they dare, I will gouge out their eyes."

"Marina!"

"Fine. If you insist on being a man about it, *you* can gouge out their eyes."

"How about we don't gouge any eyes, and we go back to my hotel room."

"Too far." Her hands worked at his pants.

"You make me do the craziest things," he grumbled, and yet his hands slid under her shirt and stroked her skin. Not that she needed encouragement to ignite her passion.

She freed him from his pants and stroked him, loving how he sucked a whistling breath through clenched teeth.

When she would have done more than caress him, he flipped her onto her back, his weight pressing her into the mats. "Oh no, you don't." His turn to feel between them, tugging at her pants. She helped him, shoving them down, an endeavor made difficult because he covered her, doing his best to ensure no one saw a thing.

The heat of his flesh pressed against her newly bared skin. The core of her pulsed with need. He teased her with his shaft, letting it slide slickly back and forth as he caught her mouth, sucking on her lower lip. Their warm, panted breaths mingled.

Excitement roared through her veins. Since he chose to be on top, that meant she could skim his frame, down the defined muscles of his back to the lean taper of his waist then the firm cup of his butt. She squeezed it then slid her hands into his pants, cupping the bare flesh.

He moved against her, once more sliding his hard shaft across her nether lips, making her hot and eager.

Their kiss had yet to end. She parted his mouth for her tongue, thrusting and tasting, enjoying a sinuous slide before sucking.

He groaned. He had a weakness for sucking.

Even though he covered her, he managed to somehow touch, trailing his fingers up her ribcage, tickling the side of her breast, nuzzling the lobe of her ear.

Whispering, "I want to fuck you."

"Then what are you waiting for?" She locked her legs around his waist, opening herself wide to him, and the tip of his cock probed the mouth of her sex. He pushed in, the thickness of him stretching her wide, but she could handle it. Wanted it. She took every hard inch and dug her nails into his back as he filled her.

She kept clutching at his back as they kissed. Their bodies rocked in time. Short, grinding strokes that were utter bliss. She moaned into his mouth. It felt so good. So right.

He ground his hips, pushing deeper, ramming the tip of his cock against her sweet spot. She clenched. Cried out.

He pushed again, and her flesh squeezed him. Almost there…

In and out. He thrust, their kiss more a meshing of breaths as they both neared the peak.

"I love you," he whispered against her mouth just as her body tensed for climax.

And she couldn't help but reply, for once. "Me, too."

It was enough for him. He came with a rough cry, buried deeply inside her, a heated pulse that brought her own pleasure. She uttered a sharp cry as the flesh of her sex undulated, shuddering around him, drawing out their bliss to a bittersweet point.

The ecstasy left them limp and entwined. She didn't want to move.

But if I don't move, then we'll be cuddling. She allowed it. Even liked it.

He felt a need to ruin it with speech. "I still can't believe Sergei is your uncle."

"I try to forget some days, too."

"He's a little crazy."

"He's Russian."

"Is he going to try and kill me for sleeping with you?"

"Possibly."

"Even though we're technically married?"

"Mostly because we're married."

"I'll hire extra security for the house then."

"When do you leave?"

"You tell me. When can you be ready to go?"

"Who says I'm going with you?"

"For one, you're my wife, and secondly, you owe me because of a certain bet you lost."

She cocked her head. "You really aren't giving up, are you?"

"No."

"Even though our lives will be fraught with danger?"

"I can't live in a safety bubble forever. Besides, I have you to protect me."

"True. And I am the best."

"Most definitely. So, what do you say, Marina Francesca Sokolov-Thorne? Will you come live with me?"

"Yes, but only because of the bet. Thirty days. Thirty days, and you'll be tired of me." Surely, their love would fade.

Thirty days later...

EPILOGUE

THIRTY DAYS LATER, AND AFTER A LOVELY WEDDING where Reaper, the stone-faced killer, actually smiled, breaking more than a few cameras...

"I am free!" Marina crowed, rolling out of bed.

Darren cracked open an eye. "No, you're not. We made another bet, remember? In the pool. Who could hold their breath longest." He was pretty sure she threw it.

"Ah, yes, six more months of torture. When will it end?" She sighed and didn't climb back into bed, rather snared his T-shirt from the foot of it and threw it over her naked body. "If I am to be tortured into living with you, then I will need food." She padded out of his room, and he smiled.

Being married to Marina definitely made life more interesting. For one, she'd made plenty of enemies during her tenure as an operative, so they'd had to work her true identity around a bit in order to give them some breathing room.

"Did we have to kill Fran in a fiery car crash?" she asked when she returned, pastry in one hand, phone in the other. "And you could have warned me about it." She pointed to the article on Yahoo pulled up on her screen.

"You keep telling me to take more initiative."

"I meant in bed," she grumbled. "Now how will I steal the latest shoes and fashions?"

"I'll buy them for you. I am rich, remember?"

"You'll make me soft," she grumbled, crawling onto the bed, her new shorter blond hairstyle a change from her previous brown locks. Until Francesca the model faded from mind, she had to sport a new look.

But that was the life of a mercenary, and she'd made it quite clear that she wasn't about to give up her job for him. However, he was determined to get her working for Harry and BBI instead of Sergei and his psycho wife. He still couldn't believe that her aunt had planned the island fiasco and the helicopter attack, along with a few other things. Now that he was family, Marina warned him to be even more alert. Apparently, dear Aunt Beth liked to keep people on their toes with surprise attacks. To hone their skills or, as her Uncle Kristoff would say, "We are taking the litter out of the house." Who knew what the fuck that meant. But everyone nodded wisely when Kristoff spoke.

"I need a new assignment," Marina announced quite suddenly.

"I thought you were about to start one that Sergei planned."

"I've decided to pass on it given the news from the doctor."

Instantly concerned, he sat straight and stared at her. "Are you sick?"

"Only part of the day. All that nausea, and then there is the tenderness in my breasts. And it is your fault." She fixed him with a glare as he took a few seconds to process her words.

"Fuck me, you're pregnant!"

"Like I said, all your fault."

"But how? I thought you said not to worry about it."

"My tracker was inside the birth control capsule, which I lost during the helicopter attack. I forgot to replace it."

"Are you okay with being pregnant?" He still recalled their awkward conversation.

"Actually, I am. It will be nice to train the next generation of assassins."

"If you're in the early stages, then you can still work if you want."

"I could. However..." Her hand cradled her abdomen. "Because of you, I now have two lines I won't cross."

And he had two reasons now to make sure Bad Boy Inc. and the academy were bigger and better than ever.

"I love you."

"Do you love me enough to hold my hair?" she said, turning green.

He did, and he even joined her in a sympathy puke.

————

THE KNOCK at the door set off his apartment proximity alarm. Good thing, because Declan slept like the dead.

The single knock wasn't repeated, so he slapped at his tablet, flashing red by his nightstand. Probably just someone coming in from a late night and banging into the walls. He'd done that a time or two. Even tried to enter the wrong apartment before.

"Waaa. Waaa."

Did someone sob?

He lifted himself onto an elbow and looked around his loft apartment. The noise appeared muffled. Was the knocker still outside his door?

Please don't let it be some drunk chick. He didn't do well with snotty noses and running mascara.

He grabbed his tablet and tapped it to bring up the surveillance camera he'd installed in the hall, only to frown. It showed nothing but darkness. Someone had blocked the lens.

The intentional act put him into mercenary mode. He swung his legs over the edge of the bed and heard it again. A little crying engine that kept starting. "Waa-waa. Waa. Waa-waa."

It came from outside his door.

He grabbed the gun from his nightstand and trod quietly in his bare feet to the portal, keeping to the side lest someone decide to blast it. It would take some pretty heavy-duty firepower given he'd had a steel-plated door put in when he remodeled the loft. The walls were thick cinderblock. He thought of it as his bunker against the world.

What he didn't understand was why he could hear someone in the hallway.

He paused by the door, arguing with himself against opening it, but that seemed cowardly. His buddy Calvin certainly wouldn't hesitate. Most of the guys he worked with at Bad Boy Inc. would fling that door open and confront what lay outside.

Probably just a drunk chick passed out in the wrong spot.

The tumblers in the many locks clicked as he turned them, and bolts slid out of their secure housings. His fingers gripped the gun tightly as he swung open the door and confronted a...

Baby?

Big brown eyes peered at him, a rosebud mouth pursed, and a note pinned to the blanket covering her said, "Congratulations, Daddy."

Declan did the mature thing, the only thing a man in his position could do.

He slammed the door shut.

THE END

Next up is Killer Daddy

For more Eve Langlais books see www.EveLanglais.com

For more contemporary bad boy romance see my new alter ego, Suzanne E. Lang at http://suzannelangromance.com/